Fiona Roberts was born in London but has lived most of her life in Poole in Dorset. She worked in the banking industry for 30 years and now runs a small business with her husband Dave.

Thank you to my husband, Dave, for enduring late dinners and unanswered questions when I was engrossed in my writing.

Fiona J. Roberts

Ebb and Flow

AUSTIN MACAULEY
PUBLISHERS LTD.

A CIP catalogue record for this title is available from the British Library.

ISBN 9781785546709 (Paperback)
ISBN 9781785546716 (Hardback)
ISBN 9781785546723 (EBook)

www.austinmacauley.com

First Published (2016)
Austin Macauley Publishers Ltd.
25 Canada Square
Canary Wharf
London
E14 5LQ

Chapter 1

The kitchen window was open allowing the smell of burnt bacon to invade the garden where Mark was trying to relax with a coffee. Burnt bacon was a familiar smell. In fact, the smell of burning food was ever present when Julia was near the cooker; Mark barely raised an eyebrow and mentally prepared himself for another onslaught on his digestive system.

Julia knew that cooking was not her forte. She was all too aware of her failings, unable to cook, nervous and tongue-tied at any social event, lacking confidence in her appearance, apart from her hair, and unable to have children. That last one, the ultimate failure, had made her a virtual recluse. The questions about having children from friends and family and the pitying looks (did she imagine them?) had taken their toll and sent her from work life to housewife, social life to stay at home and town to countryside.

They had moved into a cottage in a small village three months ago and Mark had set to work on plans for a renovation. He was an architect at Mitchell and Mitchell, a firm that specialised in industrial buildings. They specialised in creating buildings and interiors that were all variations on a theme. A lack of imagination was a bonus when working for Mitchell and Mitchell. His plan to put a large glass conservatory on the 19th century cottage, unsurprisingly, had not met with the council's approval.

The cottage had three bedrooms, one en suite, the smallest of which Julia had turned into a walk-in wardrobe. Her meagre collection of clothes looked lost in there, but what was the point of having lots of clothes if you didn't go anywhere? She could confidently say that Mark had more clothes than her. He was the epitome of the average man, medium build, 5 foot 11 and brown hair. He wore suits to work and jeans, baggy and ill fitting, at the weekend. He was not interested in his appearance which was surprising given his fastidious approach to all other areas of his life.

The rest of the cottage was cosy (small) and dated but had all the services required to make it habitable. The kitchen was old in that mismatched too much pine country style but big enough to accommodate a large tale. It had a long lounge in which they had established a formal dining area at one end. Mark had viewed it and chosen it mainly because of its remote location, which would, hopefully, give Julia the space she needed to find peace. Depression the doctor said and prescribed the standard little pills. Julia had never bothered to take them.

The depression was the result of Julia's childless state. That was what everybody who knew her concluded. Her inability to have children was the culmination of a life of relentless disappointment is what she thought. That was why she was depressed. She didn't mind being like that, people expected less of her, and that was why she never took the pills. She wasn't exactly wallowing in her misery but it did give her the excuse to not try very hard at anything. Mark was never advised that she wasn't taking her medication. He wouldn't need to worry if he didn't know.

Julia didn't care about the lack of a conservatory but she was more content since moving to the cottage which was four miles from the nearest village and only accessible from a private road. Any building work would mean an invasion of workers disturbing her precarious sense of peace. She had found that she could no longer face socialising and the location of their new home meant that she was able to avoid people for days. No one came to the door or just popped round. Their new home was small and full of character. It could do with an overhaul but she liked it as it was.

The cottage had been completed in 1856. It was built by local landowner and gentleman farmer Henry Hunter. A family of grandmother, father, mother and three children had moved in to what were then two rooms downstairs and two rooms upstairs. A fire had caused damage shortly after they had moved in and they had been forced to leave. During the next couple of years, the building was repaired and had since then been extended and modernised. It had last had real care and attention in the 1990s.

Mark and Julia had been married for 10 years. The first two years had been happy and hopeful and then less happy and hopeful with each year that passed. They were now aiming for some kind of acceptance of their childless circumstances with Mark suggesting getting a cat or a dog (too obvious a baby substitute for Julia) and then they had settled on moving to the cottage. It would be a project to occupy their time. Since Julia had stopped working she had fallen into a deep ennui and moving home was supposed to provide a focus.

Arriving at a draughty old cottage in winter had not been ideal but the arrival of spring had worked its magic and things were beginning to seem possible. Mark was enthused and drawing up plans and Julia was slightly less apathetic. She had even shown an interest in working on the garden. When Mark set off to work that morning in April Julia was clutching a trowel. She had tied her thick dark brown hair in a ponytail and strode purposefully to the garden only to be daunted by the size of the task ahead of her.

The grounds, which encircled the cottage, consisted of paving and lawn closest to the house, then some borders with overgrown shrubs and then behind them the word which sprang to Julia's mind was jungle. Brambles, overgrown hedgerows, ivy and weeds faced her. A trowel wasn't going to be any help tackling that. She had been stood looking at the garden for some five minutes now, frozen in indecision. She looked down at her feet as if willing them to move and decided, eventually, to make a full circuit of the house to assess the scale of work required. This would result in either a plan or a hasty retreat indoors and a nice cup of tea. Courage mustered the tour began and at the back of the house an area of gorse bushes and a tangle of brambles caught her attention. Tackle something hard the rest will seem easy. Where had that thought come from?

Mark arrived at work less worried than usual and was able to concentrate on his latest project. Mathematical calculations, tensile strengths, elevations, lots of straight lines, these things were soothing to him. He liked order and precision in his life and was never happier than when compiling a list or researching a project. He even liked the challenge of flat packed furniture with its instructions to follow and parts to check off. He had fallen in love with the quiet shy Julia but her fall into depression had made her almost unreachable. He was hoping that the garden would give her a new hobby.

He was an old-fashioned man in a, relatively, young man's body. He had recently celebrated his fortieth birthday. Celebrated was an exaggeration, he had gone for drinks after work with his bosses Maurice and Martin and a gaggle of secretaries. Only for a couple of hours as he didn't want to leave Julia alone and because, he admitted to himself, he didn't want to enjoy himself too much and face the guilt that followed.

The last few years had been hard work for Mark. Julia had succumbed to depression and showed no sign of recovery despite the medication. She was apathetic about everything. She didn't want to socialise or shop or cook. When Mark got the opportunity to go out he did because it helped his sanity. There were days when Julia hardly spoke at all. But he was an old-fashioned man and till death us do part and all that applied. The cottage in spring made the future seem better, yes hope was returning.

He could picture Julia when they first met. She had been shy and slightly self-conscious even then. He didn't know why, she was very attractive and had a mane of glorious dark brown shimmering hair. Her crowning glory, what a cliché but how true. She was tall but had always managed to look smaller, with her choice of plain clothes and reluctance to assert herself in any situation. He had known from the beginning that he would be the provider and make the important decisions. Now he was the provider, made all the decisions and protected his wife from the world and her insecurities. He also had to eat her cooking. Till death us do part.

Gardening gloves on and secateurs in hand Julia approached her chosen area. It had felt like donning armour and lifting a sword and now she was marching across the lawn with a sense of purpose of which she didn't know she was capable. Purpose and now contentment, she was quite tempted to let her inner smile spread to her face.

Chapter 2

The chosen area of garden submitted to her onslaught, barely fighting back with only a couple of scratches to show battle had been joined. To her delight she was rewarded with the spoils of war. An ancient water hand pump emerged from the undergrowth. It was slightly rusty but was in the ornate Victorian style and still retained an attractive quality. A salvage yard would probably pay good money for it but she wanted it to remain in place. It would be her water pump she decided and she would not share its discovery with Mark. What a thought, not sharing with Mark. She had a feeling of guilt followed immediately by a delicious glow from having a secret.

The rest of the day passed in a haze of snipping, tea, more snipping and oh my god Mark's dinner. Whatever she gave him would be microwaved, cheating but he never seemed to mind. She quickly weeded some of the border on the other side of the garden so that she could show Mark her progress. Purpose, contentment and deception.

Mark came home to a smiling Julia, that was good, news that a start had been made on the garden, also good and kitchen counters strewn with microwave food containers, splendid. For the briefest moment the word sex flickered into Mark's brain but reality stamped on that. One smile does not a sex life make, or something like that.

The rest of the week followed a similar pattern. Work for Mark, gardening for Julia and microwaved dinner. The ping that emanated from the kitchen when the meal was ready was a happy sound. It meant that an edible dinner was about to be served. Happiness of a sort had broken out and neither party wanted to break the spell but with the uncertainty of the weekend looming Friday was tense. Julia was at home thinking about the dilemma and had resolved to fill Mark's weekend with plans for the house and indoor chores. The garden would be claimed as her pet project with a strict non-interference policy applied. Mark was at work thinking he would leave Julia to get on with the garden and not interfere.

The suggestion for how to fill their weekend came from Julia and Mark was happy to comply. He busied himself around the house doing odd jobs and working on his plans for the alterations. The fact that the idea of how to spend their weekend had come from Julia was quite startling. He had been so used to her taking a back seat he sometimes forgot she may have an opinion. A moment of doubt about their new found happiness arose when he saw the beef joint on the counter and realised home cooking had returned but he chose to count his blessings. What would it be today? Undercooked or overcooked?

The hiding of the pump had been foremost in Julia's mind and so, after the initial pruning, she had moved behind the pump close to the fence and cleared it from that side. A screen of shrubs remained in place protecting it. Mark would have to push through brambles after walking through a border to find it. The pump could be seen from the field behind the cottage but she had never seen anybody there.

So what now? The pump was exposed and the next thing would be to try it out. A hint of worry surfaced, she could feel her brow crease and negativity creep in. Would it work? Would the water be foul? Try it, what is the worst that could happen, positivity asserted itself. She put her hands on pump and began work. There was creaking, resistance, anticipation and after some toil some water. Water tainted by rust and dirt but increasingly clear until it looked thirst-quenchingly good to a suddenly thirsty Julia. Scooping it in her hands Julia slaked her thirst with the sweet tasting water. She had done it, anything was possible now.

Chapter 3

The small improvements Mark had noticed in Julia's confidence and therefore her mood seemed to continue. She smiled when she talked about the garden and her plans for it. The real revelation was some three weeks after the gardening began when a plate of edible, he would even go as far as to say tasty, homemade food was presented one night. This led to a great deal of inner turmoil for Mark on what his response should be. Too much praise would be patronising. Saying nothing was an option but that could be hurtful too. His final solution was the comment, "maybe you should cook this again...sometime". Julia was amazed.

The first meal Julia had made for Mark when they started dating was an unmitigated disaster. Since then she had improved slightly to the point where things were mostly identifiable and just about edible. That was if she kept it simple. If a dish had more than half a dozen ingredients all bets were off on the result. A well-thumbed stock of takeaway menus was available in case of catastrophe. Julia's mother appeared to be afflicted by the same bad cooking curse. Julia was the middle one of three sisters. Her older sister Kelly was confident and focused.

She wanted a career and she got one. She wanted a husband and she got one. She wanted a child and she got two! How efficient of Kelly to have twins so that she could avoid the trouble of going through pregnancy twice. The younger sister Sarah was the problem child. Hair dyed a strange colour. Check. Tattoos. Check. Single parent. Check. She was always asking their parents for money and they were always handing it over. Julia would never ask her parents for money. Julia would never ask her parents for anything.

Between praising Kelly and despairing over Sarah her parents had little time for Julia. It didn't matter though because Julia was fine. That was the consensus. Not good or bad just fine. As a child Julia had realised it was nearly impossible to command her parents' attention when she wasn't as driven as Kelly or as wild as Sarah. There was no resentment from Julia of her lot in life. She had accepted her mediocrity, never totally admitting to herself that it was an excuse to coast through life. The first time she had cooked for Mark had been a disaster, he didn't seem to mind, so why make an effort to change? Her mother was equally inept at cooking and it had never bothered her father.

Over the last few weeks Julia had achieved things. Gardening and cooking. She had been sleepwalking through her own life. She had been neither happy nor unhappy and now she was in a race to catch up for lost time. It now mystified her that she had not tried new things.

Maybe she had really had depression and was now recovering. Her new problem was how to fit everything into her busy days. More gardening, researching and trying out new recipes, venturing to town not just to the village, specialised ingredients were required for her cooking, and pumping water for her personal consumption.

There was a downside too. Self-awareness was wonderful but having confronted herself and set out on a course of remedial action, her attention turned to Mark and thoughts of what he needed to change. A list was forming in her mind. A long list. First of all, she had to address his clothes. The somewhat baggy faded jeans and collection of

18

golf style jumpers made him look older than his years and if he was updating his wardrobe surely she could do the same. If she could get him to be less uptight with his attire maybe it would filter through to other parts of his life. She could transform him but she realised that subtlety would have to be employed. Carrot not stick. Sex?

If Mark was being manipulated, he didn't give a damn. The resumption of marital relations had coincided with more suggestions and input from Julia on a range of subjects from the renovation of the house to recipe ideas to what he should wear. When had she started noticing that? When had he last cared what he wore? The only child of older parents Mark had grown up in a stultifying atmosphere. There were no arguments or raised voices or overt demonstrations of affection in the household. They had moved into what was essentially a retirement bungalow in their fifties. They were preparing early for their deterioration. Mark's 'style' was therefore understated to the point of bland and more suitable to a man of sixty. He was not exactly repressed but he was uncomfortable with emotions being overtly on display and particularly disliked any form of disagreement.

He had left home to go to university and had briefly flirted with the wild side of life. He had a couple too many drinks on occasion but no drugs. A few dates with women who he was assured would 'put out' but he found that distasteful. He soon realised that he wanted a career, a wife and a family in that order. Anything else was a distraction. He had hardly played the field when he met Julia but he knew she was the one.

A Saturday had been set aside for a trip to town so that they could both update their wardrobes. Mark had made a list of what they needed and Julia had looked it over and decided to ignore it. They shopped, some unexpectedly, and to Mark, disturbingly fashionable clothes had been purchased. He was now the proud owner of a hoodie. The name of the thing disturbed him let alone wearing it. He had suggested they call at the village pub on the way home, he needed a drink after spending all that money, and Julia had agreed.

Mark had occasionally visited The Green Man when sanctuary from the world (Julia) was needed and had met and chatted to a number of their neighbours. Although Julia used the Post Office and the mini supermarket in the village she had not really explored anywhere else or sought out any potential friends. Her modus operandi in public spaces had been head down, please and thank you in the shops and then get the hell out again. On that day she noticed the red brick community centre with its notice board advertising such wonders as Pilates classes and yoga as well as the usual scouts, girl guides and mother and toddler mornings.

The village was nice but the addition of new buildings in the sixties and seventies made it not the chocolate box ideal that people longed for. The price of property compared to other local villages was therefore more reasonable, a large consideration for Mark when buying the cottage. Apart from the shops and the pub there was a bed and breakfast which incorporated a restaurant and a pretty church which seemed to be unused. Some enterprising developer would no doubt turn it into a residence. Executive homes had been built on the outskirts which increased the number of people using the village's facilities.

He was nervous about taking Julia to the pub, she wasn't good in a crowd, but she suffered all the introductions with a shy smile and even had a glass of wine. She knew next to nothing about wine and mentally put that on her list of things to investigate. The visit to the pub hadn't been as bad as Julia had thought it would be. Usually she could feel her face burn with embarrassment and her tongue tie itself in knots when meeting a stranger. She had felt slightly uncomfortable at first but had soon, surprisingly, relaxed.

Chapter 4

Hard work and attention to detail had once been important to Julia. When she had a job she had been very conscientious and the firm of solicitors for whom she worked were sorry to see her leave. An employee dedicated to her work, not partaking in office gossip or drinking too much at office parties. She was ideal. Since giving up work she had not really made much of an effort at anything.

The old determination returned and her hard working methods were now applied; to her, gardening and wine were not therefore just dallied with they were disciplines to be mastered. Books were bought and the internet trawled, the more information the better. Julia now had a folder to keep all her recipes in and dozens of pages were bookmarked on the computer. Mark was glad that she had new interests and glad that she discussed them with him of an evening in the cosy living room, after the increasingly good meals eaten in the kitchen around the old pine table.

She still sought Mark's advice. "Do you think we could go to the garden centre at the weekend? Am I being too ambitious trying to make a curry?" He found himself admonishing her for doubting her skills and encouraging her to try new recipes. His stomach no longer churned with dread at smelling something foul emanating from the kitchen which he was expected to eat. Now his return from work was stomach friendly.

Mark arrived at work now with a spring in his step. His newly stylish appearance, lighter mood and the chats with the staff had made him more popular around the office. The pink shirt which he wore caused a sensation. Maurice and Martin, the Mitchell and Mitchell of the business's title, were grey or beige, in every way, and glanced nervously at the PAs and secretaries lest their heads were turned by this dazzling display. A certain amount of interest from young Lucy was flattering to Mark and a great ego boost but that was all. Was this some kind of women's intuition or pheromones which made Lucy's flirting coincide with his much improved home life (sex life). The irony was not lost on him.

Julia had read a great deal about wine in the last couple of weeks and was now ready to introduce a daring new concept to Mark. Wine with their evening meal. Just a glass so that she could choose her favourites. So that they could choose their favourites. That evening she said, "I am cooking sea bass tonight so we will be having a white wine. Sauvignon Blanc." Had Mark been a cartoon his eyes would have popped out and his jaw hit the floor. The sea bass was perfectly cooked and the wine perfectly chilled. A second glass? Why not? Who knows where all this could lead, thought Mark praying for sex with the lights on. He did not know what was happening to Julia but he thoroughly approved of it.

"I've researched a bit about gardening and it's too late to plant shrubs so I'm focusing on getting some colour. We need foxgloves, nasturtiums and godetia." Julia was pushing the trolley. Julia seemed to be in charge. "You can get the heavy stuff, potting compost, two bags and we'll need some nice pots. I'll choose those." Mark was faintly amused, or was that irritated, by the competent Julia. Check yourself, he thought, what a relief it will be to have some of the decision-making load taken off his shoulders.

"Do we want any garden ornaments?" he ventured.

"No, too twee. I don't want anything twee." This from a woman who still had all of her childhood stuffed toys and drank tea from her favourite mug with the kittens on it. Although he couldn't remember seeing that mug for some time now. He had agreed to the garden being her domain but surely he could make the odd suggestion. Maybe the suggestion could be considered not dismissed out of hand. He put a small dog statue in the trolley anyway and Julia pretended she hadn't noticed.

They called at The Green Man for lunch on the way home from the garden centre. Julia commented on the limited menu and wine list, but conceded that they were aiming for pub grub not gastro. "We should go into town for a meal next week. I need to see what the latest food trends are."

"Shall I book somewhere?" Mark asked.

"Wait until I've gone online and read the reviews. I'm getting into food now and want to try the best." Fine thought Mark, knowing that the best would also be the most expensive. This dining out was not becoming a regular event. He would put his foot down. Mark was as careful with money as he was with other aspects of his life. They didn't go without but they were not extravagant. Julia had never shown an inclination to buy lots of clothes (until now) or demand luxuries thank God.

In the garden Julia was making great progress. She had chosen pots and planted them with flowers. They were now scattered around the paving at the back of the house. The borders had been tidied and she had attacked more areas with her trusty secateurs. She had placed the statue of the dog in the border opposite the back door. It made her smile each time she went outside.

That night they were going for a meal in town. Julia had found a restaurant that looked good and she had read the menu online over and over again. She was excited to eat some real cordon bleu food and hadn't even worried about going out in public. She had new clothes and was looking forward to wearing something dressy; she lived in jeans, and had been practising walking in her high-heeled shoes. Mark was suitably complimentary when he saw Julia in her blush pink dress.

Le Chaudron was everything Julia had hoped for in a restaurant and everything Mark dreaded. A menu where the descriptions of the food were sprinkled with French and dripping in pretension. For starters Julia ordered the soufflé au fromage with salad featuring pommes et noix. Mark had the pate, or, as per the menu, pate de campagne with a shallot confit followed, of course, by the chateaubriand (very expensive). Mark prayed for full tummies and no desserts. Julia read the dessert menu with relish. "Profiteroles, I love those. Oh, pear tarte tatin, charlotte a la framboise, I wish I had some room but I'm stuffed, I mean full." Mark began to breathe again. Mind you the damage had mostly been done. Especially when you added in the sommelier's recommendation of a bottle of Margaux. He had indigestion.

Chapter 5

Julia said, "I've had an idea." That comment would once have been received by Mark as a revelation but was now a cause for concern (fear/expense).

"Go on, share."

"Well now that I'm more confident with cooking I thought we could have a small dinner party. Perhaps with Maurice and Martin and their wives."

Mark replied, "If you think it's not too much for you." Pause. Long uncomfortable pause.

"What exactly do you mean by that?" Julia was speaking in a precise clipped way.

"Oh I'm sorry that came out the wrong way, I meant don't go to too much trouble or make it too formal. I know Maurice and Martin are old-fashioned but I think they prefer informal." Stop talking, Mark told himself. Julia retreated to the garden and found herself taking a long fortifying drink of water using the metal mug she had hung from a chain on her pump.

Diaries were consulted and a date booked for a Friday at the beginning of June. Julia made lists. A shopping list. Wine list. Household chores to be completed. Jobs for Mark to do. She was like a general planning a military campaign. And she was good at it. She promoted herself to a five star general. After much consideration the menu was settled upon.

French onion soup with croutons. A classic which could be prepared in advance and then reheated. Beef Bourguignon and mashed potatoes, a lot of preparation but impressive results.

For dessert crème brulee which always looked so good in those little dishes. Cheese and biscuits. Cheddar, for Maurice and Martin and stilton and brie for the others (her). A Pinot Noir would be served with the main course, a Sauternes with dessert and port with the cheese. Julia would sip judiciously throughout the meal so that she could retain her composure and be the perfect hostess. She had never really been a great drinker and was surprised at how much she had enjoyed the wines she had tried so far.

Mark was given the more mundane tasks. Touching up paintwork around the house, shifting furniture, polishing silver (didn't butlers do that?) and some food tasting which was the best bit. He felt a glow of pride when he watched Julia performing her alchemy in the kitchen. It was taking a while for him to adjust to the new Julia. He repeated his mantra, "Change can be good," several times and tried to relax and accept the new status quo.

The kitchen was no longer a place that filled Julia with anxiety. The many unused utensils which had been bought and put away were now found and employed. The knives, peelers, pots and pans and wooden spoons felt comfortable in her hands. The oven which had spewed out so many burnt offerings had now been tamed (there were other settings than high apparently). At times as she moved around she almost felt as if someone else were doing the cooking. Mark was smiling as he watched her kitchen ballet.

When the evening arrived they stood hand in hand beside the beautifully laid pine table smiling in anticipation of their guests' arrival. Neither of them could quite believe that this was happening. Julia cooking for a dinner party. Julia socialising. Julia enjoying cooking and socialising. The table looked like a photo in a magazine spread. A table runner ran along the length with a modern candelabra in the middle. Wine glasses, water glasses and a jug of water. Polished cutlery and white linen napkins, totally impractical but very stylish. The plates and serving dishes, white with a simple silver stripe at the edge, would finish off the 'less is more' elegance.

Julia was wearing a dove grey wrap dress and she had chosen blue trousers and a blue and white checked shirt for Mark. She wore stud earrings and a small locket and chain and just a trace of makeup. Working in the garden had given her a light tan and she was feeling and looking good.

Maurice and Ann and Martin and Christine arrived at 7.30pm precisely. They were in their mid-fifties, Maurice was the older of the two brothers by two years, but dressed like people in their seventies. The brothers were in suits and ties and the ladies were arrayed in clothes featuring various shades of brown. An unlikely calm had descended on Julia. She had walked around the garden before their arrival and refreshed herself with water from the pump. Mark was also calm. Julia's serene smile and air of confidence were rubbing off on him.

After a quick drink on the patio everyone took their places at the table at 8.00pm, as planned, and the first course was served. The Mitchells were plain eaters and were aghast at the notion of soup with a floating island of cheese on toast in the middle. "Delicious" said Maurice.

"Can I have the recipe?" said Ann. Martin and Christine wondered what was next.

"Beef Bourguignon, how clever you are," from Martin. The compliments were coming thick and fast now. In the kitchen in between courses Mark had warned Julia not to be too specific about the ingredients included in the dishes. Maurice and Martin, it seemed, were terrified at the mere idea of garlic. There would be much talk later that evening and the next day in the Mitchell households about how much Julia had changed and how happy she and Mark seemed.

They had met Julia at one previous Christmas party a few years before. Since then Mark had attended functions on his own. Julia had been ill at ease (miserable) at the party and had not participated in any of the conversations. They had never tasted her cooking before but Mark had regaled the office with many a story of her culinary disasters. What had caused such a marked change?

When dessert was served the guests had to find new superlatives. The little ramekins holding their golden contents were placed on the table and everyone just stared at them with a kind of reverence. They had to be urged to break the crisp top with their spoons and discover what lay underneath. The cheese board was viewed with some alarm by the Mitchells who eschewed the more exotic selections in favour of the cheddar.

"So, what plans do you have for the house then Mark?" Maurice asked.

"I would like to extend but it will have to be done sympathetically. The conservatory idea was a nonstarter as far as the council were concerned. They didn't like the UPVC or the size. Maybe I'll have better luck with wood." Steel, plastics, breeze blocks and concrete were the tools of the trade as wielded by Mitchell and Mitchell. Martin wasn't sure how Mark would get on working with wood and had to stop himself recommending he employ another architect.

"And what about all that garden? I wouldn't know where to start," said Christine.

"Well I'll refer that one to Julia, she is the gardening guru." Mark nodded to Julia to take up the baton.

"Oh I don't know that I'm a guru," laughed Julia. "I have bought some gardening books and done some reading. At the moment I'm just tidying things up. I'll be planting more stuff in the autumn and might try some vegetables next year."

Good food and good conversation. Julia didn't need the wine and the port, she was on a natural high. The meal could not have gone better. The others had all had a few drinks. Just because she was being careful didn't mean that there wasn't plenty of drink for everybody else. At the end of the evening Julia and Mark watched their guests walk slightly unsteadily to the taxi with everyone vowing to, "Do it again soon." Mark turned to Julia with a glint in his eye and she took his hand.

Chapter 6

July arrived and Julia, body confident, could be found sunbathing in a bikini in the garden. A jug of her freshly pumped water was on hand to keep her cool. For a couple of weeks after the dinner party she had basked in the glory of her success, but now she needed something more. An impatience was building about what that more should be. She had welcomed inertia for so long and now she could not bear to be without a challenge.

Mark would have been happy to remain in the post dinner party bubble. He had never loved his wife more or been so content. Once again his affable demeanour was catnip to Lucy, who volunteered to take post, tea, pens and whatever else he needed (or didn't need) to Mark. He was so focused on Julia now that he no longer even noticed Lucy, who with her blonde hair, curves and wicked laugh was the antithesis of Julia.

It now felt to Julia that she had just toyed with cooking and gardening and wine. One of the problems was that she had only Mark to bounce ideas off and with whom to discuss things. His air of contentment was great but it had made him almost too agreeable. She longed for him to question her or play devil's advocate instead of all the nodding and smiling. She was tempted to throw in an outrageous suggestion just for the shock value but she couldn't really do outrageous. Another thing to work on.

Since giving up work Julia had lost contact with the couple of friends she had. Moving to the cottage meant that she was more isolated than ever. She had relied on Mark for everything but now realised that she needed female company. She imagined herself having coffee and trading recipes with a few close friends. Maybe she and her friends would go to town clothes shopping or have a girls' night at the pub. Where would she find these longed for friends? She remembered the community centre and the classes on offer.

The Pilates class was on a Tuesday at 11am. Research had revealed that specialist clothes were needed, so a trip to town had been necessary to buy the leggings and t-shirts which were somewhat expensive for clothes in which to sweat. A conversation with Mark about her allowance would have to be sooner rather than later. Still emerging back into society Julia had agonised over being the new girl at the class and how to maybe make some friends. She wouldn't be pushy, well she couldn't if she tried, she would smile and say hello. Small steps and after a week or two she hoped to at least have traded names and, "What terrible/good weather," type exchanges.

Julia's friends in the past had been of a certain type, glamorous and socially confident, in whose shadow she could hide. Now she didn't feel so much like being a shadow person. Basking in the spotlight would be too much but she wanted more than a walk on part, at least a line or two. Due diligence would have to be done on the prospective friends so that she didn't revert to her old bad choices. A list of questions, interview questions, formed in her mind on that Tuesday at the end of July when she approached the community centre.

The village was of a classic commuter belt type. Middle class women with middle class neuroses would be in attendance at the Pilates class. Would it be like her schooldays with the bitchy clique and the glamour squad and the also rans (her)? Julia was less intimidated than anticipated and smiled and hello'ed her way through the small group. So far so good. Jo, the instructor, toned and predictably upbeat insisted on making her stand at the front and give a brief resume by way of introduction. Initially mortified Julia could see that this was a convenient shortcut in the friend-making process and found herself giving a Miss World type address. "My name is Julia I live just outside the village with my husband Mark, who is an architect, and I enjoy cooking and gardening," (nothing about world peace).

There were a few older ladies at the back of the room, more talk less exercise, a couple of grimly determined ones at the front, more exercise no talk, and the middle occupied by, well, the middle. Julia headed for the middle. The pack of five in the centre were now, unknowingly, candidates for Julia's friendship.

Donna was small and round. She wore the tight workout clothes, not seeming to care that every bump and overspill was on display. She welcomed Julia after the others had spoken, sharing that she wasn't very good at Pilates but needed some me time away from her four young children. She had the distinctive accent of a village local.

Zoe had been the first to talk and that had been an indication of her alpha type personality. Small and compact she had stood, feet apart, in front of Julia fixing her with an unnerving stare tempered slightly by what could loosely be described as a smile. "Just relax and follow Jo, but if you need help just ask me. I've been coming here since these classes started and I'm a bit of an expert now." Zoe then launched into an introduction of her own which was rapidly turning into her entire biography. Thankfully she was distracted momentarily and Julia escaped.

Behind Zoe, Emily and Claire rolled their eyes and barely suppressed giggles. They were younger than Julia and were obviously firm friends. Their sleek highlighted hair and designer gym clothes were like badges displaying their middle class credentials. It came as no surprise that their husbands worked in the city and that they each had young children. Did they also have dogs, Agas, and a secret drink problem? Julia would henceforth think of them as the clones.

That left Faith. She was 35, slightly younger than Julia who was 38, and was of average height and build and quietly confident. Zoe had slotted Julia in between herself and Faith and the class began. Faith was attractive and understated. She had light brown hair and wore no makeup unlike the clones. She smiled and said hello to everybody and seemed to be well liked.

Having tea and biscuits (somewhat counterproductive) after class gave everyone, who wanted to, a chance to mingle. Zoe monopolised Julia's time giving her helpful, to Julia baffling, advice about Pilates and fitness in general. She also resumed her biography picking up at the point she left off, university, and moving on to her career in PR. She spotted Claire reaching for a third biscuit and broke off her speech to point out the number of calories and the amount of fat in it and Julia managed to escape. She circulated as much as she could, fending off the usual questions about children and accepting compliments about her lovely hair. She had known that the children thing would happen and faced it with a new-found bravery. Faith found Julia and congratulated her on giving Zoe the slip and, having asked the "Have you any children?" question, didn't overly sympathise or gush awkwardly in an attempt to change the subject. Faith had one child, Freddy who was six, but definitely didn't want any more.

Julia and Mark had visited doctors and consultants and fertility clinics in their efforts to have children. The problem, they were advised, lay with Julia who had felt guilty of depriving Mark of a family since the diagnosis. They had tried a round of IVF but the physical and mental strain had been too much for her and they had reluctantly agreed to not try again. Julia had been dismayed at the first failure and felt that she couldn't cope with another potential disappointment. Mark had wanted to try again but seeing Julia so distressed he had backed off and accepted her decision. He wondered to himself sometimes what family life would have been like but they never spoke about it again. Another problem wrapped up in silence and put away.

Faith was patently the front runner in Julia's search for a best friend. The Goldilocks of friends, not too shy or too forward, too dull or too glamorous and not prone to talking constantly about her child. She had known that type with their, "Maisie is walking and she is only nine months."

"Oh Archie was running by then."

"My Callum was playing football at 10 months and is now signed to Chelsea." Competitive mums; she wondered if she would have been like that.

Chapter 7

Julia had made a plan and she was determined to stick to it. Despite Faith's seeming suitability Julia did not want to jump in too quickly so it was on her third visit to Pilates class that she asked Faith if she would like to come round for coffee some time, perhaps, if she was not too busy. Faith reached for her phone, consulted her planner and after much clicking and browsing said she was indeed free and would be available between the hours of 11 and 2 on Wednesday and Thursday of the next week. "Well pick a day and let's make it lunch shall we?" Julia boldly asked.

More planner consultation and then Faith declared, "Wednesday at 11.30 then."

Mark was thrilled when Julia told him about her new friend. "What are you going to make for lunch? Don't intimidate her too much with your skills or you won't get an invite back." These were words she never thought she would hear concerning her cooking.

"I'm going to keep it simple. A chicken Caesar salad and a glass of white wine."

"Very nice. Now that's made me hungry, what's for dinner?"

"Just a beef goulash," said Julia.

Early August and the garden was full of colour and the day was warm. Julia had wiped over the patio furniture and set it for lunch for her and her friend Faith. The salad was made, with a homemade dressing of course, the wine was chilling and a jug of tap water was on the table. The pump water was only for her and she had drunk a fair amount of it that morning during her preparations. Everything was ready by 11.00 so she sat in the sun in smart shorts and T shirt and had a small glass of wine to toast herself.

Of course Faith was on time. Julia had chosen well. "Your cottage is so charming. I didn't even know it was here."

"That was part of the attraction really," Julia confessed. "I like going out or having people round occasionally but I like my own company. People don't just pop in if you are out of the way." Faith agreed that uninvited guests were a pain. They were sympatico.

There was at ease in each other's company and Julia found herself telling Faith of her problems trying to conceive and how that had affected her self-confidence. Faith reassured her that everybody suffered low self-esteem at some time in their lives (probably not Zoe) and moving to the village and living in this beautiful setting was surely beneficial. Julia agreed that something about the place was special. Faith had struggled to conceive too and had just been lucky when she fell pregnant with Freddy. Like Julia she was not prepared to put herself through the trauma of trying for another child. She was determined that Freddy wouldn't grow up as a spoilt only child.

The lunch went well, not that Julia was worried after their initial chat, and after a tour of the house and garden Faith suggested that the Wednesday lunch date become a regular thing alternating between their houses. "Don't, whatever you do, tell Zoe." Faith cautioned. "She so thinks that she is the boss of me and that I'm helpless without her." Zoe was the self-appointed ruler of the middles and felt it was her duty to meddle in all their lives. She meant well but she had an unfortunate lecturing manner. Faith occasionally fought back, Donna let it all wash over her and the clones laughed their way through everything. Julia had another secret now about the lunches, how exciting.

Julia had never had secrets before. Now she had the pump to conceal from Mark and the lunches to hide from Zoe and the other Pilates ladies. Of course there were other secrets she kept but they didn't really count. Those were about her feelings; everybody had secrets like that didn't they? On reflection they were not so much secrets but thoughts that she had no idea how to express. They were about her life, her family and Mark. Would she ever be able to say the things to other people that she needed to say?

Mark was enjoying work now, rather than just turning up and switching to autopilot. He was relaxed, that was the reason. He was secure in his position at the firm, not yet a full partner but that would surely follow, and part of him had accepted the simplicity of the designs on which he worked. He was no Richard Rogers and had no desire to be. Ambition was relative and his stopped at being a partner. He was never going to be an innovator. He found a beauty in the buildings he designed. Others may not see it but practicality, affordability and functionality were pleasing to him.

His ambitions for the cottage had also changed. The need for bigger and more modern accommodation had faded with Julia's appreciation of what they already had. Did they really need more room? Maybe he was looking at the impression the house would have on others, not what they actually needed. The garden and cooking took up a lot of Julia's time now and he found himself, instead of renovating the house, napping in the chair on a Sunday afternoon like an old man.

He and Julia had met her friend Faith and her husband Alex at The Green Man one evening for drinks. They were good steady people and Mark was happy that Julia had made such suitable friends. Should the occasion arise he would be glad to introduce them to Maurice and Martin. Alex was an accountant and he and Mark held a conversation which to the uninitiated sounded as if it were conducted entirely in some sort of number code. Alex mentioned that he was a member of the local golf club and asked Mark if he ever played. It was something Mark had thought about but not pursued.

The girls weren't taking any notice of the men; they were happily engrossed in a bit of Zoe bashing. She had fairly barked at Julia and Faith in last week's Pilates class, "Will you concentrate and try to keep up." Emily and Claire were red-faced with the effort of suppressing their laughter rather than the effort of the exercise. Was her irritability a sign that she was suspicious that Julia and Faith were meeting behind her back?

At the class Zoe had questioned them both about their movements in the previous week much in the way a policeman would conduct an interview. Julia and Faith had got their stories straight and were not going to crack under the pressure. They would have to be careful what they talked about when she was around. Julia had forgotten what it was like to have a friend. She had never really been part of a group of friends. The machinations of a group dynamic were slowly being revealed to her.

Donna stood back and observed. She was the only one of the 'middles' who had been born in the village. These people with their 4x4s, competitive dinner parties and not just keeping up with but outdoing the Joneses and then rubbing their noses in it, why did they bother? Some might say that she couldn't compete and had therefore given up. She was sure however that she had a better life than them even taking into account the chaos of four young children, offset by the joy of course, and the lower household income.

Julia had never previously felt competitive due to her general apathy. Alas her awakening did not confine itself to positives and she was quickly becoming acquainted with the seven deadly sins.

Pride, yes she spent far too long choosing her outfits and styling her lustrous hair. Anger, well that was summed up in one word, Zoe. Greed, she liked pretty things, could a woman have too many clothes? Gluttony had come with the cooking. If only she wasn't so good at it (pride again). Envy was a permanent state in her 'I want the best' world. And lust, yes there was lust. Mark was a happy man. No sloth for her though. Being driven by all the other sins did not give much of an opening for sloth. She was envious of people who had time for sloth.

Mark didn't think of himself as a mean man, just careful. Looking through the bank statement had, in this month of September, not been pleasant reading. Julia wanted more clothes. Julia spent more on food. Julia needed a larger allowance. Julia now went to a beautician! "You don't want me to look shabby when I see my friends do you?" Mark's rictus smile didn't waver in the face of Julia's artfully crafted question. "And you love the dinners I cook now. I don't hear you complaining about the wine either." Game, set and match. Mark would have to think of a new tactic before he broached the subject again. He was beginning to be nostalgic for the days of apathy.

A wine rack had appeared in the kitchen, a very large wine rack which was full. As Julia found new recipes she took to the internet to see which wine was the perfect accompaniment for the dishes. It might recommend a Chablis but which was the best Chablis? It was only through trial and error that she would find the ones to her taste. She was buying a lot of wine. Some of the ingredients appearing in the cupboard were fairly exotic too. Surely they didn't need all those herbs and spices?

Julia had upgraded her exercise clothes to a fashionable, more expensive, make. A more expensive make than the ones worn by Emily and Claire. The smiling clones stared, huddled and discussed and smiled a little less brightly. She wondered when they would upgrade. Faith was a little surprised by Julia's purchase. She had thought that Julia wasn't the type to be drawn into the whole one-upmanship thing. She imagined that following her self-imposed social exile Julia was anxious to impress.

They had enjoyed a couple more lunches since the first successful time at Julia's cottage and it was now Faith's turn again. It had become apparent that a quick sandwich and a cuppa, her first offering, was not going to cut it. Julia's second turn had produced a quail's egg salad with boudin noir. Why couldn't she just say black pudding? Faith set out for the deli in town. Faith knew that she could not compete with Julia's cooking. Anyway she had Freddy to look after and couldn't spend her days looking at recipes and crossing the county to procure the rarest ingredients. Boudin noir for heaven's sake. She was not going to be caught up in some escalating cook off. Roast dodo anyone?

Good ingredients were Faith's answer, hence the visit to the deli. She had bought a selection of meats, olives, sunblush tomatoes and artichoke hearts. These items had been decoratively arranged on a large platter. Tiny bread rolls, carbs were the enemy, were in a basket but no butter was to be seen, fat was also the enemy. Faith was not serving wine, drinking during the day and then driving to pick up Freddy was a no-no.

Julia arrived dressed as though she was attending a garden party with the Queen. A short strappy brocade dress and vertiginous sandals. The question "What no hat?"

rattled around in Faith's head but fortunately remained inside. No alcohol was offered just tea or squash or water. Julia wanted wine or her special water. She would have to get through this lunch fairly quickly so that she could get home and crack open a bottle.

The table in Faith's kitchen looked pretty in a shabby chic kind of way. The food on the table was looking more than pretty it was looking good. Julia was seething. Clever, clever Faith, acknowledging her limitations with cooking but working round them. She didn't even question her furious reaction to her friend.

"This looks, nice." Julia had chosen the word nice and delivered it with the slightest hesitation. Perfect. "Where did you buy," (stress on the word buy) "all this lovely food?"

"It comes from Deli Delight in town. Do you know it?" asked Faith.

"Yes of course, but I prefer the one run by Italians off the high street. Massimo, the owner, imports directly from all over Europe. Such a nice man who has helped me get the more unusual ingredients I need for my gourmet cooking."

Julia picked at the food. It was all quite delicious but she couldn't bring herself to say so. She made insidious comments such as "How unusual" and "I don't normally have this sort." A last minute softening somewhat salvaged the situation. "Next time at mine then. How am I going to dream up something to compare to this?" In Faith's mind there was still a little too much ambiguity in those last words.

Why had she been so angry about Faith's lunch? Julia mused on her response and bitchiness. She had always been the underdog, the follower and now she wanted to assert herself more. The fact that Faith had upstaged her and not even cooked anything was cheating she decided. Her reactions had therefore been perfectly justifiable in the face of such underhand tactics. She would forgive Faith this time. It never occurred to her to question her own behaviour.

Chapter 9

When Mark arrived home Julia gave him the details of her lunch with Faith. "No cooking was involved. Just stuff bought and plonked on a plate. Well not plonked, it was arranged quite nicely, but no cooking!" She didn't mention the lack of alcohol. She had noticed Mark frowning when she reached for the bottle of wine of an evening.

"Julia, not everybody has the expertise in the kitchen that you have. I hope that you were tactful about it."

"Of course I was, you know me." Not so much these days, thought Mark.

Julia was still wearing the brocade dress and Mark had wondered why she had gone so over the top for a lunch date with a friend. He had never known her to be competitive before. In fact, she had been the opposite of competitive (whatever that was). Maybe it was her lack of confidence that was making her overcompensate. She was being a bit waspish about her friend Faith as well. "So what are you going to make next week? Maybe you should dial it back from the boudin noir." God, what was wrong with people? If you've got it flaunt it. Somewhere deep, deep down in the place formerly inhabited by Julia's conscience something stirred. It was uncomfortable and made her feel bad. She would be trying to ignore that in future.

Faith was also discussing the day's events with her husband giving a blow by blow account of Julia's gibes. "Are you sure you weren't imagining it?" asked Alex. "She was so nice when we went to the pub for drinks."

"The person I met at Pilates just a few weeks ago is not the Julia I saw today." said Faith.

"Are you going to hers next week?"

"Oh yes, she was probably just having an off day or I'm being too sensitive. Although if she carries on like this I might be running back to Zoe!" Faith tried to rationalise Julia's actions. She was not used to social situations so maybe she was experimenting with boundaries. She hoped that sense would prevail and Julia would calm down.

Julia didn't like being made to feel bad by other people's petty insecurities. Her confidence was soaring and she wouldn't be dragged back down. These twinges, these feelings would have to be quashed. She felt better after a walk to the pump, a good glug of water and a couple of glasses of wine from the bottle she had hidden under the sink for emergencies.

Mark had annoyed her this evening with his 'Dial it back' comment. What did he know about the politics of ladies who lunch? So she didn't know that much but it was more than him. Now however she was going to have to play nice if she was going to get sex. The effort she had to put into everything. Ever more exotic meals, a clean and stylish home and cosying up to Mark. All of these things were chores. She felt a strange nostalgia at times for her do nothing days but soon shook it off. Life was revealing new possibilities and new experiences and she was going to try them all.

So she needed something to lighten her mood. Julia planned a trip into town the next day for some clothes shopping, fast becoming one of her favourite things.

Unfortunately, she had blown through her allowance spending a ridiculous amount on that workout gear. Mark was, well he would say, 'careful' with money. There was no chance of snaffling his credit card or slipping a few notes from his wallet. It would have to be window shopping.

The walk-in wardrobe (third bedroom) was now filling up with Julia's new clothes. Beautiful clothes in beautiful subtle colours. Grey, plum, sage green, soft pink and more grey. The brocade dress was a bit jarring amongst the muted palette. In the corner on an old rack Mark's unironed shirts hung limply. He was getting up earlier in the morning to do his own ironing now. He felt that he couldn't complain in this age of equality so he internalised his displeasure. When did hobbies take precedence over household chores?

He was selecting his shirt one morning when he focused more on his surroundings than usual. The rails were fairly full, he had expected that after reading the bank statements. The door of the wardrobe behind the rails, he noted, had burst open. Further investigation revealed piles of clothes with the labels still on. No time now but after work he would have to delve deeper into this.

At work Mark was distracted by the discovery of the wardrobe full of more clothes. Clothes that hadn't even been worn. He was impatient to get home and investigate further. He didn't mind Julia buying clothes (he did) but if she had so many that she wasn't even bothering to wear some of them then it was becoming a problem. He had coped perfectly well with a minimum wardrobe for years. Why did she need all that stuff? And the shoes, ridiculous. He thought of the hoodie which had been flung over the rail and never worn.

That evening, whilst Julia was in the kitchen, Mark went to the spare bedroom or as he was later to think of it, the scene of the crime. Some of the expensive clothes in the wardrobe, so casually tossed in the bottom, didn't just have labels on they had security tags too .It took him a moment to realise the ramifications of what he had unearthed. He tried to think of a reason why the tags were there. Maybe the shops had forgotten to take them off? There were far too many items for that to ring true and he had to face the facts. They were stolen. By Julia.

Much of their marriage had involved burying their heads in the sand rather than confront their issues. Much of Mark's life had been the same. His parents never argued they simply ignored any problems holding their resentment inside. Mark sat on the floor in front of the wardrobe shocked by what he had discovered and horrified by the fact that, this time, he would have to do something about it.

Mark girded his loins and, grasping a security tagged silk blouse as evidence, marched into the kitchen. Julia was aware of his presence but she was busy cooking. His silent unmoving figure at last piqued her interest and she turned to look at him. The speech rehearsed by Mark ready for the great confrontation was never delivered. Julia saw the blouse in Mark's hand and knew she was in trouble. Mark was scowling, he never scowled. There was only one thing she could do. She cried.

Chapter 10

The previous avoidance of strife in their marriage meant that Julia had never had to turn on the tears before. She was a natural. The small sobs and gasping for breath. The pitiful glances from under tear-soaked eyelashes. The pitiful glances that registered Mark's anger and then his gradual softening. The crying had bought her time to collect her thoughts and invent an excuse. It may not stand up to close scrutiny but Mark seemed shaken enough by her display to buy it.

"I feel so terrible about this. I'd shut myself away for so long and I couldn't believe that I could make friends. That people would like me. They're all so well dressed. I wanted to be like them, be accepted, but I couldn't keep spending all your money." Stop, now wait for a response from Mark. The excuse had come to her quickly. Deceit was a useful tool she had discovered and so was crying. New exciting revelations every day.

"How long have you been stealing?" A rather harsh word for Mark to use she thought. In her view it wasn't stealing, although she hadn't come up with an alternative description yet.

"The last couple of weeks. I'm sorry I knew it was wrong but I was desperate."

"I hope to God you weren't caught." said Mark.

"No." Julia didn't think that adding how good she had become at shoplifting was appropriate.

Why had she started shoplifting? For Julia it had only partly been about the acquisition of new clothes. She needed excitement in her life after the years of inaction and had wanted to really feel alive in a way she had never experienced before. Danger had provided the jolt she required to kick-start a new life. A life in which she would experience new things, taste new food, make new friends and not be afraid any more. A drastic start she had to admit but if she could do that what adventure would she be able to undertake next?

There had been moments in Julia's brief criminal career when she had come close to being caught. In her instance stereotypes were on her side. She was a smartly dressed woman and therefore not immediately under suspicion. A slightly confused look followed by abject apologies had got her out of a couple of awkward situations. Everybody was so busy in the modern world it was easy to believe that she had forgotten to pay. On the whole walking out with her chosen item had been relatively simple.

There followed the predictable "I know you won't do this again" and "What were you thinking?" comments which Julia sniffled pathetically throughout. Oh well, it had been fun while it lasted. The terrible excitement as she adopted the 'butter wouldn't melt' expression, which had got her out of a scrape or two, as she headed for the shop exit with her illicit stash had been wonderful. The clothes were a bonus. She had nearly been caught a couple of times and was even followed everywhere by security in one shop now. The decision to give up her life of crime had all but been made and Mark's discovery was the final nudge.

All things considered it had turned out better than expected. The use of crying had been tried and proved successful. Julia, who had never lied before, found the use of guile relatively easy. She also had a wardrobe full of clothes she hadn't paid for and the beautiful twist was that through her tears she had negotiated a raise in her allowance. Rather than being chastened she was emboldened for her next venture.

Chapter 11

The lunch this week was at Julia's. Autumn was setting in so the colder weather gave her the opportunity to make homemade soup. It was an easy recipe, for someone of her skill, but it was still more of an effort than Faith had made. The minestrone soup was made and bowls and cutlery were on the table. No pretty mats and napkins today. Julia was getting bored with cooking now that she was so good. Where was the challenge? Where was the competition?

Not coming from non-cooking Faith. She was so organised too. Everything done by 10.45. She had sampled her water throughout the morning now for something a little stronger.

Sauvignon Blanc had been her first experience of wine and her taste for it had not dimmed. It was so crisp and refreshing. She had flirted with Chardonnay, Pinot Grigio, Viognier and more but always returned to her first love. She selected a large glass and filled it to the brim, took a large gulp and topped it up. Saves walking back to the fridge again, she reasoned.

When Faith arrived Julia had already consumed two large wines and was just pouring her third. Faith had not been looking forward to their lunch after the last time. Today however Julia seemed more relaxed and the lunch seemed like it would be less formal. Julia's clothes were definitely less formal, a pair of jeans and a silk shirt (that silk shirt), but still made a statement. That statement being 'Look at me, this is dressed down and I'm still fabulous'. Her constant hair flicking was beginning to grate.

After fifteen minutes Faith had been given a cup of coffee but now an hour later there was no sign of food. "Oh my God. I've been banging on and you're just sat there starving." Faith had finally prompted Julia who was now stood in front of her range cooker, wine in hand, stirring (poking?) the soup.

"Well at least it's worth waiting for." She was happily squiffy and fairly slopped the soup into bowls and wobbled to the table the contents sloshing precariously from side to side.

Faith wolfed down her soup, yes it was nice, and got the hell out of there. Julia had been on the way to being drunk when she had arrived at 11.45. What time had she started? The conversation, details of Julia and Marks' sex life, had been excruciating. She couldn't wait to tell Alex. She wasn't sure whether she wanted to carry on with the weekly lunches, although this one had a certain cringe worthy entertainment value. She would see what happened at next week's Pilates class.

"She was drunk by twelve o'clock. Are you sure?" Alex was incredulous.

"By the time I left she was unsteady on her feet." Faith was discussing the lunch with her husband. The unnerving thing about it had been Julia's utter lack of concern. She hadn't tried to hide her drinking or pull herself together at any time. The bottle was on the table and when it was empty she simply got another one. Tuesday 11.00 Pilates class. Julia knew she had been drunk last week and knew she had maybe been too candid about things but she was finding it hard to be embarrassed. It had been fun, a new experience. She didn't have to brazen it out in front of Faith she simply didn't care. She breezed into class, wearing makeup, and tossing her hair with not a care in the world.

Faith had been tempted to share all with the 'middles' but that meant Zoe finding out about the lunches. Alex had cautioned against gossip. "Mark would be appalled if he found out what she's been saying." He was right, of course, but his warning about spending time with Julia had only worked in the reverse psychology sense making her determined to try lunch again.

No apologies were forthcoming from Julia. She strolled across the room greeting the girls and nodding at the older ladies as usual. She flicked her hair again. Throughout her life people had complimented her hair. She wore it in a variety of styles now not just pulled back into a ponytail. Plaits, hair bands and hair clips in bright shiny colours now adorned her mane. She gave it another flick and pulled it back into a ponytail before they started.

How would Zoe have reacted to Julia's performance? She would probably, after a long stern lecture, have dragged her to the nearest AA meeting. The clones, as Julia called them, were almost certainly secret tipplers themselves so the story would be lost on them, Faith reckoned. Donna's opinion was more difficult to gauge as she had a live and let live philosophy. Somehow she was cocooned from the outside world, strolling through life unperturbed. Donna had her problems but nothing that couldn't be surmounted by a good frank discussion and, the great panacea, tea.

During the tea and biscuit session after class Faith finally got to talk to Julia and felt that she had to address the debacle of last week's lunch. "Yes I was a bit drunk. I've never been drunk during the day before. You've got to experience new things. Makes you feel alive." Julia was unrepentant. "I had to throw together a risotto for Mark's dinner and then feign a headache so that I could go to bed." she laughed. "I will endeavour to be sober when I come to yours next week." she said with a mocking sincerity.

"When you go to Faith's next week!" Zoe appeared over Julia's shoulder with a look that could curdle milk.

Chapter 12

The cat was out of the bag. What was it about Zoe, so small in stature that made Faith and Julia hang their heads like naughty schoolgirls? "I went to Julia's last week for lunch and she's coming to me tomorrow," confessed Faith. Julia was happy to be complicit in the lie that last week was the first time.

Zoe simply stated, "I'm free tomorrow." Their fate was sealed.

Julia managed to dredge up a, "The more the merrier," in response and a quick I'll phone you signal to Faith behind Zoe's back. Faith had no choice, faced with Zoe's glare, but to invite her. Julia had made a hasty exit and now she was left to take the brunt of the fallout. "It sort of happened once and then I had to invite her back" Faith explained. Zoe didn't look convinced but she had an invite now so let the matter drop. She had known Faith and Julia were up to something.

An hour later, "I know, I know. What could I do?" wailed Faith before they both giggled hysterically again. Julia was on the phone finding out what had happened after her hasty exit. Faith and Julia had decided to see the funny side of the situation and embrace their (unwanted) guest as best they could. Any differences had been put aside united as they were against a common foe.

"Has she asked you what she should wear?" enquired Julia.

"No, but it doesn't matter because she'll be right and we'll be wrong." Cue more uncontrolled laughter.

"What are you going to make? May I suggest humble pie?"

"Good one. She's so strict about her diet, I might just pile the table with cream cakes and see what shade of purple she goes." Faith and Julia were having far too much fun at Zoe's expense.

Faith presented chicken and sweet chilli sauce wraps at lunch the next day. It had been great fun to fantasise about playing cruel tricks on Zoe but she would never carry it through. Her conscience was in good working order and had been wagging its finger at her in admonishment. She even bought some fresh fruit and put it in a bowl to convince Zoe that she had a healthy lifestyle. The effort was better than facing a lecture about her diet. Julia was a little disappointed not to see the cream cakes.

Zoe was her usual self, a bit bossy and prone to lecture, the nutritional value of everything they ate was provided by her, but Faith wasn't unhappy about her presence. She had a sobering, in every way, effect on Julia which made the lunch a far more civilised affair. They ate, drank tea and coffee and listened to Zoe. The lunch was declared over when Zoe checked her watch and announced that she had another very important appointment. "Come along Julia, let's leave Faith to it. Freddy will be out of school soon."

Zoe thanked Faith for her hospitality and said how much she had enjoyed it. "Where's the next one?" she asked. Julia said that she would host next time, which Zoe was thrilled about as she was longing to see the cottage. Zoe marched Julia to the door and added, "Thank Faith for the lunch Julia." Julia fumed all the way home. Zoe had monopolised the lunch and ordered Julia out of Faith's house at least an hour before Freddy was due home. Why had she let herself be bullied like that? It was like having a bad flashback to previous pushy friends.

In college Julia had been friends with a girl named Hilary. She thought they had been friends but she was more like Hilary's lackey. They went where Hilary wanted to go and listened to music Hilary wanted to listen to. When Julia had met Mark her friend's reaction had been pure fury. Who would she go out with now? Whose homework would she copy? Recognising that she had been used had been devastating for Julia.

As usual at times of stress Julia headed for the sanctity of her garden gravitating naturally to the pump and a cooling cup of water. Frequently these days the trip to the garden was followed by a trip to the fridge where the wine bottle awaited her. One glass to relieve the tension she told herself. A couple of hours later she was still drinking. A vague nagging feeling interrupted her drinking briefly. What was she supposed to be doing? She chose to ignore it.

Mark wouldn't be getting his dinner that evening.

Mark had not been fooled by Julia's headache ruse the week before. She had been tipsy. After the shoplifting revelation Mark couldn't face another confrontation and reverted to ostrich mode. Head firmly buried in the sand. So she had drunk a bit too much wine. It was ladies' lunch day at the cottage and she hadn't had to drive. Since then there had been no recurrence and Mark was glad he had been spared from dealing with that problem. He had been spared for a week anyway. The sight that greeted him on his return from work was Julia slumped over the kitchen table, still holding her wine glass, snoring. He didn't know whether to laugh or cry.

He made a vat of coffee and shook Julia awake. She glowered at him like a sullen hormonal teenager. "My head hurts," she moaned.

"Yes it's called a hangover. Drink your coffee and then we need a serious talk." Mark had aimed for a sanctimonious tone and he was spot on. Julia sighed. Mark was sat opposite her at the table with a look of saintly forbearance. God she could slap him. Her head was pounding, all she wanted to do was lie down. She thought about crying again but didn't have the energy. Mark's parochial view meant that drinking during the day was practically a mortal sin. How was she going to get out of this one?

Julia would blame someone else. She would blame Zoe. "She bullied me. It was like being at college with Hilary." Zoe had been the cause of her tension so there was an element of truth. "After all the progress I've made I was right back there in English class. Completely dominated, not allowed an idea of my own." Now she had to apologise. "I know that drinking is not the answer. I'm really, really sorry."

"But this isn't the first time you've been drunk during the day is it?" asked Mark. She thought she had got away with it last week. Damn it.

The temptation to scream was almost unbearable. Bloody Mark. Julia took a deep breath but her mind was too befuddled to think of an excuse for the time before. So she cried. The sobbing and another couple of cups of coffee delayed the resumption of the talk. There was not enough time in the world, though, to come up with another reason for her behaviour. Julia liked doing whatever she wanted. In the past that had been not very much. Then she had enjoyed cooking and gardening. Now she liked drinking.

Julia adopted the appropriate contrite demeanour as Mark talked. He was concerned, it wasn't like her, what could he do to help? Blah blah blah. "You're silly to drink with the antidepressants you take too." He still thought that she was taking them. Why didn't he notice that she had never taken them, but spot the drinking? Julia realised something. She was going to have to be a great deal more careful in future. Mark was going to be watching her more closely now. He was her husband and, more importantly, her provider so she would lay off the wine for a couple of weeks and prepare some lovely food. She would be the dutiful wife.

She was definitely on a learning curve. Julia had never had the inclination to tell lies or engage in subterfuge but she now found these things to be necessary. It was a challenge to think up excuses and hide things and at the moment she was finding it rather exciting. Mark had been so trusting that it was relatively easy to pull the wool over his eyes. Up until now anyway. Lately he was noticing too many things and was proving to be more troublesome than she had anticipated. She wouldn't underestimate him again.

If only she could get to the pump and get some water, that would make her feel better. But Mark had made her go to bed, even tucking her in, and had promised to look in on her throughout the evening. The water would get rid of her hangover. Whenever she drank the water from the garden she felt better physically and mentally. The last time she had been drunk the nausea and headache had been instantly relieved by it.

Mark was as annoyingly reliable as ever. His head appeared round the bedroom door on a regular basis and he came in occasionally to adjust the quilt. Julia would have found it quite nice if she didn't have such an urge to get out of the house. It was October now and she was loth to make a midnight run to the pump in the cold autumn air but it looked like that was the only opportunity she would get. Fate intervened and she fell into a fitful sleep and the pump was forgotten. She didn't wake up until after Mark had left for work. She ran down to the pump in her dressing gown and slippers and applied her remedy.

Operation good wife kicked in after several glasses of water. Laundry, cleaning, shopping and ironing. Julia was glad to have lots to do she was trying to occupy herself. Tonight she would cook Mark's favourite, cottage pie. Not one of her cordon bleu dishes but he liked it. Try as she might to distract herself, Julia was unsettled. She had an itch she couldn't scratch. It wasn't about the drink, that had been fun but she could go without it. (Couldn't she?) It was about freedom. Her lack of freedom. Society had rules, she knew that, but arse to them if they got in her way.

She had always been a good girl. Julia had seen other people be rude, queue-jump and other crimes (she had considered them crimes in the past) and had been appalled. She reconsidered people's behaviour now and thought that maybe they were just asserting themselves and being honest. What was wrong with that? Another excuse for another aberration.

Mark was glad to see a sober Julia when he came home from work. When he had changed out of his suit he had seen the rail of freshly laundered and ironed shirts. Dinner was cottage pie which he recognised as a peace offering and accepted it with relish. He shouldn't complain, there had been obvious improvements, but Julia had an attitude. Small things caught his attention. The pause before she answered his questions, just enough to indicate irritation with him. The glass of water heavily banged down next to his plate. The silence during the meal. Julia knew how to play the game however and at the end of dinner produced a dazzling smile. "I hope you enjoyed that. I know it's your favourite." OK, he would hold his tongue, this time.

Chapter 13

As Mark settled in front of the television that evening he thought back over his life with Julia.

The early days when he couldn't believe his luck at having such an attractive wife. The first home festooned with cushions and flowers and ornaments. Then the frustration in their attempts to conceive and Julia's resulting depression. The way Julia dealt with any problem had always been to repress her feelings. Quiet withdrawal. Despondency. It was not healthy, he knew that, but it was how she coped. The dramas of the last few weeks were completely out of character for Julia. Mark felt seriously out of his depth. Nobody who had met his shy conservative wife in the past would have predicted her becoming a shoplifter who drank to excess. Nobody who had been subjected to one of her burnt meals would have foreseen the improvement in her cooking.

Mark tried to pinpoint the time when these changes had started to occur. He remembered her seeming to awaken from her torpor at the beginning of spring. How hopeful he had been back then seeing her smile again. He thought of the marvellous meal they had had with Maurice and Martin and wished that they could go back to that time. He realised that Julia had never had a rebellious youth. His had been very short lived but hers was non-existent. This was her version of teenage disobedience. It was just twenty years too late.

The days of denial about their problems had been easy when they were both playing the same game. Julia had changed the rules and Mark now had to have the arguments he had always avoided. Julia's petulant display could be accounted for by being hungover so there would be a stay of execution this time. He was rapidly running out of delaying tactics and braced himself for the next drama.

They had moved a hundred miles away from their families years ago. Seeing her sisters have children was torture for Julia, as much as she loved her nephews, and her parents were preoccupied with the grandchildren. They were practically raising Sarah's son. Mark's parents were now in their late seventies and seemed content as they meandered around their bungalow barely communicating. Nothing new there. At this point Mark wished their families, however dysfunctional, were closer so that he had someone with whom to share his troubles. He thought about phoning one of them but couldn't decide who would be able, or willing, to help.

Mark's parents Bill and Margaret wouldn't be able to comprehend the change in their suitably shy and decorous daughter-in-law so he couldn't turn to them. Bob and Penny, Julia's parents, were seemingly incapable of any kind of discipline. The word no was not in their vocabulary. Kelly and Sarah ran roughshod over them all the time. Sarah had more bad habits than Julia so she would be no help. Kelly was a very competent woman but was always busy running her sons' and husband's lives. If push came to shove he would enlist Kelly.

Chapter 14

When Mark was at work he tried not to imagine Julia at home guzzling wine. He had selected a new notebook from the stationery cupboard and would use it to document Julia's misdemeanours. Anything out of the norm would be noted and he could then stamp on any worrying trends before they became entrenched. He kept it in his briefcase and hoped he would not have to use it too often.

"Have you been rummaging around in my cupboard?" Lucy was leaning over the desk and Mark was trying to avert his eyes from her chest.

"I didn't know I needed permission," joked Mark.

"You must always ask a lady's permission." It was a bit like being in a Carry On film but it was good to have a light-hearted exchange.

Mark smiled "I solemnly promise, henceforth, to ask before I rummage. Would you be so kind as to let me keep the notebook I took from stationery?"

"For you, anything."

Maurice was hovering at the door. Mark didn't know it was possible for a man to purse his lips so much. "How's Julia?" he said pointedly.

Lucy made a rapid exit clutching a folder for effect. "She's very well thank you."

That was a lie. Mark spent much of the rest of the day thinking about Lucy. It was pure fantasy. He was 40 and she was 23. He was married. Till death us do part.

So far in Mark's notebook he had written the word 'Drunk' with the dates of the last two Wednesdays underneath. 'Shoplifting' was another heading and written below was 'No recent evidence'. He had reluctantly included a section for behaviour and had recorded Julia's sulking after being caught drinking. It was being picky but he had written 'Laundry' noting that this week it was satisfactory. He was on a roll.

The big test would be the following Wednesday when the next ladies lunch took place. Mark was tempted to speak to Faith and Zoe and ask them to keep an eye on Julia. It would be the sensible thing to do but, luckily, he decided against it. He wasn't in tune with women in general (not many men were) but something prevented him from making the mistake of telling her friends about her drink problem. Faith already suspected but if Zoe knew nothing would stop her from making Julia's sobriety her personal crusade.

Julia was not looking forward to lunch with Faith and the interloper. She was caught between wanting to impress Zoe with her culinary skills and not bothering at all. Good old pride beat sloth. A chicken and sesame stir fry, made in front of them, would do the trick. Flinging colourful ingredients into a wok describing the stages of cooking like a TV chef. She would be putting on a show and keeping Zoe quiet. Still being on the alcohol ban she would serve Chinese tea in little oriental cups.

Zoe arrived and took a self-guided tour of the cottage, rifling through cupboards and drawers as she went. Faith and Julia watched her with amazement that she could be so brazen. In a strange way Julia admired her approach. Whilst the inspection was going on Julia suggested that Faith and her husband join her and Mark that weekend for a meal out. Faith consulted her planner and said a provisional yes, babysitter permitting.

"Very nice," was Zoe's appraisal of the cottage. "Obviously you've still got a lot to do to the place." She then reeled off a list of jobs that needed doing. She even offered to write them down, in order of priority of course.

"Thank you Zoe." This being nice to people was really starting to grate on Julia, but she was on probation at the moment so had no choice. The bloody list was going straight in the bloody bin.

"Take a seat at the counter ladies and I'll make lunch." Julia smiled and launched into her performance. "As you can see the vegetables have been cut to a uniform size." She had the floor and wasn't going to give it up. When Zoe tried to query something it was met by, "Any questions at the end please." After Zoe had gone Julia apologised to Faith. "I know I went on a bit but it was a way of keeping Zoe quiet. Saturday will be so much better with just us and the husbands." Will it? thought Faith.

Chapter 15

Faith and Alex suggested the Hunter House restaurant in the village. It was a good local eatery not as upmarket or pricey as Le Chaudron so Mark was happy. "This place used to be the home of the local squire I think," Faith said.

"I don't know much about the history of the village considering we've lived here for four years. Donna from Pilates is the one to ask. She was born in the village, as were her parents and grandparents. Probably a few generations before that as well."

The restaurant had indeed been the home of Henry Hunter. It was now run as a boutique hotel, the locals called it a bed and breakfast, and the dining room was open to the public. It had been a grand Georgian house and the owners had restored it faithfully. The restaurant was a wood panelled high ceilinged room and Julia entered excitedly looking around. The venue was so good and the evening had so much promise and then the menus were handed round.

Julia was disappointed to see the conventional food on offer. Pate, prawn cocktail, garlic mushrooms and the entrees, steak with various sauces, a chicken dish, a salmon dish, she could have made them at home. The others were discussing their choices while Julia sat back sulkily. There was nothing even vaguely interesting available and she wasn't going to pretend that she was happy. On top of that Mark had told her before they left home that she was only allowed two glasses of wine so this was going to be a long evening.

"Have you decided what you're going to have?" asked Alex.

"Oh I'll let Mark order for me. The menu is so limited I can't really work up any enthusiasm."

An uncomfortable silence followed. "The pate is very nice," offered Faith.

"When you make your own pate so well why would you order it in a restaurant?" Julia replied. Julia then read out the entrees. "Pan fried salmon with capers. Made it at home. Spinach stuffed chicken breast. Made it. Steak Diane. Made it. Made them all and probably better than here."

"Well," said Mark. "Here you don't have to do the washing up."

Alex and Faith were open mouthed with horror. They went to the restaurant on a regular basis and were extremely embarrassed by Julia's statement in front of the waitress. Poor Mark shared their discomfort.

The rest of the evening was a masterclass in carrying on in the face of adversity. Everyone, except Julia, dug deep into their 'Let's be British about this' reserves and soldiered on. Julia made no further contribution to the conversation but showed her displeasure in a series of sighs and eye rolling. Mark moved the wine bottles away from Julia each time the waitress topped up their glasses to stop her helping herself to more. It was like a bizarre game of chess being played out on the table. Mark ended up paying the entire bill in atonement. That made him even more unhappy.

Alex turned to Faith when they got in the car and said, "Never again." She couldn't really argue with that. The whole experience had been awful. "Thank God she wasn't drunk," he added. "She was loud enough as it was with her criticism, if she'd been overheard we'd never be able to go there again." Faith had been angry with Julia's behaviour and wasn't even going to try to defend her.

Later, when they got home, they had discussed events further. Alex declared that Julia had some sort of mental problem and pretty much forbade Faith from having lunch with her again.

"What on earth made her act like that?" Alex asked. Faith tried to think of any reason for Julia's behaviour. She tried to think of any clue that she was even capable of that kind of behaviour. Drunk outrageous conversation and a bit of competitive cooking had not presaged the mega sulking which had ruined everyone's night. She would have preferred the drunkenness to the sinister undercurrent that had pervaded the evening.

"I don't know what she was thinking. It's as if a new Julia emerges each time I see her. And each one is worse than the last."

Mark was furious. He was unused, and averse, to displays of emotion but the last few weeks had changed that. "Do I have to explain to you how rude you were?"

Julia shrugged, "Do you think they'll want to go out with us again?" Shrug. "Do you have anything to say?"

Julia turned to him and shouted, "YES. SHUT UP." So that is exactly what Mark did. He barely said a word to her for the rest of the weekend.

Julia didn't look particularly ashamed of her behaviour. And she was wearing that stolen shirt again. When Monday morning came around he found his shirts had been ironed and his lunchbox had homemade quiche inside. The beginnings of a rapprochement perhaps. Once again Julia had managed to head off a confrontation. Mark was becoming more and more concerned and more and more bemused with every incident.

The Pilates class would be interesting Julia thought. She, once again, was shameless and wanted to hear what Faith would say. Not very much it seemed except to inform her that she would be unavailable for lunch for a while. Oh please yourself thought Julia. Why should she pretend she was enjoying herself when she wasn't just to keep others happy? The middles were quickly aware that something was amiss and Emily and Claire asked subtly probing questions as Donna looked on.

Zoe, typically, was more forthright. "Why aren't you coming to lunch tomorrow Faith? Have you and Julia fallen out?"

The other middles froze waiting to hear any explanation. "Um we're just having a break for a while. I've got a lot to do," mumbled Faith.

"Oh well. Julia you're still coming to me aren't you?" Zoe enquired.

Julia turned slowly to look at Zoe. A malevolent look on her face. "Actually I would rather go to the dentist and have all my teeth pulled than be stuck one on one with you." Open mouths and gasps. "You only want someone there so that you can talk at them. On and on about fitness and calories and other shit that no one's interested in. Also..."

"Enough." Donna was the one to step into the fray. "Let's all calm down. The class is starting any minute. Work out some aggression with exercise and sort it out after with a cup of tea." As much as Donna believed in the efficacy of tea she doubted that it would work this time.

During the class Julia had time to reflect on her hot-headedness. She would have to back down to some extent or she would never be able to come to Pilates again. She debated the situation with herself. Stick to her guns and become a social pariah or apologise. She was seriously considering the former (what she had said was true) and then an excuse formed in her mind. She was getting good at them.

"Zoe. I had a mega migraine on Saturday when I saw Faith so I was completely out of sorts and as a result we've fallen out. It's upset me terribly and I'm afraid I took it out on you." No one was entirely convinced but an effort had been made and a grudging truce was called.

After Julia had left Faith turned to Zoe and said, "That's the first I've heard about a migraine." Faith outlined to the rest of the middles what had happened when they went to dinner at the Hunter House and a discussion ensued.

Faith felt uncomfortable like she was telling tales but Julia's conduct at the meal and at Pilates needed to be talked about. She mentioned Julia's drinking too. Everyone had a say. Zoe had been the victim and was unhappy at Julia's verbal attack but pointed out that they didn't really know her and therefore couldn't judge whether this was her usual behaviour or an aberration.

Emily was prepared to give her the benefit of the doubt as was Claire. Donna wondered what had made Julia act that way and reminded them that their first impressions were of a quiet shy person. They agreed to give her another chance.

Chapter 16

Back at home Julia quickly forgot about the row. She had come up with an excuse, if they chose not to believe it so what. She decided to refocus herself on her hobbies. There wasn't that much she could do in the garden at this time of year so she picked up a recipe book and looked for something exotic to make. The following Friday evening, having shopped for ingredients, Julia presented Mark with a lamb tagine. The wine she was serving, after researching the best accompaniment, was a Rioja reserva. Her week had been spent making small gestures of penance to Mark. They were now managing to have conversations which consisted of more than a couple of words.

The tagine was delicious and Mark and Julia found themselves able to smile again. The wine had helped. Julia's new tactic was to keep topping up Mark's glass so that he would become tipsy and not notice her own drinking. (Genius). This was followed by a chocolate and banana bread pudding served, of course, with a dessert wine. Julia was full up but she brought out cheese and biscuits so that she could have some port too. Mark had been vaguely aware of the amount of alcohol that they were consuming but he needed to relax as well. When Julia suggested a brandy though he summoned up the willpower to say no, although she managed a small glass in the kitchen whilst she was clearing up.

It was November now and cold. They lit the log burner most evenings in the cosy living room and tiptoed around each other preserving the fragile peace. The cold snap had driven Julia inside and she had therefore visited the pump less. She often found herself stood by the kitchen window looking across to where it was hidden. She always wanted to drink the water but running across a rain-lashed garden did put her off.

The last couple of months had been crazy, Julia could see that now. Her conscience was growing again and was nagging her about past behaviour. She would have to do some serious bridge building with Faith and the other middles, including Zoe whom she still couldn't feel that bad about. She found paper and pen and began making a list of ways to rehabilitate herself. Making a list made her smile. Whatever happened in their lives Julia and Mark always made a list.

When Julia attended Pilates class next she didn't have to affect a shameful look, she felt it, a bit. Faith and the others noticed her contrition and softened slightly. Nobody knew what demons were eating at Julia although they all had problems. Rumours of Julia's drinking had spread throughout the class and mooted as a reason for her rudeness. They hadn't known each other long but Faith felt that she should have a heart to heart with Julia. Maybe her antics had been a cry for help.

"Let's skip the tea and biscuits and go to the cafe for a chat," Faith offered. They sat at the back of the room nursing skinny lattes and after the usual preliminaries, family, weather, friends, Faith ventured, "I've been worried about you, the drinking and well you know."

Julia sighed. "I know. I'm sure at this point I should give an explanation or an excuse but I just don't know what I was thinking. I was doing things that just weren't me. But I didn't care."

That was true she didn't care. Then. Now Julia looked back and saw what had happened as if it were happening to someone else, a bad version of Julia. Poor Mark, how bemused he must have been. And she'd told him to shut up. The drinking to excess hadn't helped. Oh God, shoplifting. "Please forgive me Faith. I know that I have to prove that I've come to my senses and I appreciate you giving me a chance. Poor Zoe, she was finally lost for words." They were laughing again.

Faith and Julia discussed their lives from childhood troubles to their current midlife anxieties. Faith was not surprised at the stories of Julia, the middle child, being lost somewhere in the family drama and her gradual retreat into herself in the last few years. They were all reasons for why she had been so erratic recently. Julia was obviously remorseful for what she had done but still could not really explain her personality change. Faith thought that Julia should make an effort with the middles to get them back on side

The next week Julia invited all of the middles to a pre-Christmas lunch. After planners were consulted they agreed to meet at the cottage the following Monday. A secret Santa present giving was hastily arranged and a spending limit set. Everyone left kind of appeased and hotly anticipating the lunch.

Chapter 17

Julia's need to show off had subsided so the lunch wasn't going to be some fancy grandstanding event. She was preparing a buffet. Crostini with salmon and cream cheese and with beef and horseradish. Chicken satay, prawn vol-au-vents and humus and crudités also featured. Something for everyone she hoped. There were soft drinks for everyone but also a bottle of Prosecco to give proceedings a festive feel.

Emily and Claire fairly skipped into the house, excited to be invited and anticipating, hoping for, a bit of drama. Usually only seen in gym clothes they were eager to display their style. Emily wore skinny jeans, blue, boots and a pale blue cashmere jumper. Claire wore skinny jeans, black, boots and a pale pink cashmere jumper. At least the colours were different.

Donna was delighted to be invited to the cottage. She had been in the house when she was a child but had not seen inside since. At that time the place was owned by an ancient man referred to as Uncle Sam. Other people had lived there since and had made renovations. She arrived wearing baggy mum jeans topped off with a Christmas jumper featuring a snowman.

The jumper made everybody smile and so set the perfect tone for a relaxed lunch. Faith helped Julia in the kitchen and Zoe praised the food, although she couldn't stop herself entirely from voicing her worries about the calorie and fat content of some of the items. She ate a lot of crudités and just one vol-au-vent.

Donna mentioned that she had been in the cottage before and they were all interested in how the place had changed. It seemed that it was much smaller back then, the two storey extension was added later. As a child she and her mother had visited a man known to Donna as Uncle Sam although he wasn't a relative. Her mother had been friends with his wife. She took him casseroles and pies and the occasional cake. Uncle Sam had finally moved to a warden assisted flat when the remoteness of the cottage proved to be difficult. His wife had died at a relatively young age, before Donna had been born, and her mother had kept an eye on him after that.

The secret Santa present giving took place as the Prosecco was served. Faith received a voucher for the beauticians in town (from Claire). Zoe got a smoothie maker (from Julia, who was still feeling guilty and exceeded the spend limit). Emily got a set of designer hair products (from Faith). Claire got a set of designer cosmetics (from Emily). Donna got a smart workout T shirt (from Zoe). Julia was thrilled with her present (from Donna) which was a book on the history of the village and featured old photos of her cottage.

Mark arrived home to find Julia slumped in a chair in the living room. His initial concern was allayed when she got up, smiling, to greet him saying "I'm exhausted. I so wanted today to be a success and it was. The food, the presents it was great."

"I'm glad you had a good time. No ramifications from recent events then?" asked Mark.

"No, thank God. Do you mind if we have takeaway tonight?" They hadn't had a takeaway for so long Mark had to hunt high and low for the menus. The dinners Julia cooked had been excellent if increasingly outlandish. He would not have dared suggest a takeaway and for her to do so was another indication of her positive change.

The Mitchell and Mitchell Christmas soiree, as Maurice insisted on calling it, was coming up soon and Mark had been fretting about taking Julia. He retrieved his notebook from his briefcase and reviewed the contents. Julia had not been nasty drunk for a while. The shoplifting appeared to have been a one off. His laundry had been done and she had not told him to shut up again. All in all, a marked improvement in her behaviour. He would be happy to take her to the party but would still keep an eye on what she was drinking.

Christmas would be spent at Julia's parents' home this year. Mark had also worried about that. What would the family think of Julia's drinking and swearing? He had never previously heard her raise her voice and he doubted that they had either. He knew it was always a testing time for her surrounded by her nephews and upstaged by Kelly and Sarah. If they could keep on this even keel everything would be ok. He would keep an eye on her drinking there as well, mind.

One step at a time, the party first. A sort of trial run for Christmas day. If it looked like she was backsliding Mark may have to cancel Christmas. There was an appeal to spending the day at the cottage shut away in the warm. A long drive to the coast in winter was never his first choice but they had a duty to her parents. And his parents too. They would of course be expected to visit. They would endeavour to squeeze some conversation out of them whilst drinking a cup of tea in the cloying heat of their bungalow.

A possible bonus of the Christmas trip was Julia's recently found cooking prowess. If Mark could get her into the kitchen and distract her mother, they might actually get something edible. No wonder Julia had been such a bad cook; her mother's cooking was of a similar quality.

Chapter 18

The Mitchell and Mitchell soiree was being held at a hotel in town in a small function room.

Maurice and Martin were old-fashioned gentlemen and this meant that the buffet and drinks were paid for by them. It was their obligation. They viewed the staff in their office as an extended family but still retained an archaic formality when dealing with them. As owners of the business they were never addressed by their first names. Unknown to them around the office they were referred to as Mitchell one and Mitchell two.

Their dated views extended to the arrangements for the Christmas party. There was no disco or entertainment, the buffet was meagre and the drinks limited. Those who had attended in past years were aware of the shortcomings and had called at a local pub first to pre-load on booze. Mark had declined the offer to join the secretaries and office juniors, mindful of Julia and her propensity for wine. He also had an eye on his future with the company and wanted to ensure he was being considered for partner.

They arrived at the party at 8.00pm to find only Maurice and Ann and Martin and Christine here before them. "I said 8 o'clock. I don't know where everybody is?" Maurice fretted. In the Fox and Hounds was the answer. Julia was wearing a silky shift dress with sequins around the neckline. Although the dress was black and demure she still looked like a bird of paradise next to Ann and Christine. Calf length polyester wasn't a good look on anyone.

"In the new year you must come to us for dinner again," said Julia.

"Oh that would be lovely it was so good last time," Ann replied. "I must apologise for not inviting you back but we've now got my elderly mother living with us and it makes things so awkward."

"And we've been having an extension built on the house which seems to be taking forever, so that has ruled us out too," added Christine.

At 8.45pm, Maurice noted the time, the rest of the party arrived. Four giggly secretaries and their partners, the accounts manager and his wife, the office manager and her husband and the new trainee and Lucy. Seeing the look of disapproval on Maurice's face provoked a chorus of apologies and over the top praise of the setting, the buffet and the wives' dresses. The buffet was a sea of beige. Sausage rolls, finger rolls with egg and ham, chicken nuggets, crisps, nuts, quiche and daringly some samosas. Still beige though.

Julia looked at the buffet and smiled. Bad Julia (she had given her alter ego a name) would have thrown a fit faced with this lot. The house white and house red wine wouldn't have gone down well either. She had received compliments on her dress from the others that were a lot more sincere than those directed at Ann and Christine. She smoothed her hair, the flicking had abated, and looked around the room.

What was that young blonde girl wearing? thought Julia. Lucy was in a red dress that barely covered her. The Mitchells would have shown disapproval if they weren't trying so hard to pretend that they hadn't noticed. Mark had noticed. He had also noticed that Lucy had arrived with Simon. She had made an ostentatious show of hanging onto his arm and gazing up at him as she passed Mark. She was now feeding him sausage rolls from the buffet. An occasional glance in Mark's direction was made to ensure he'd seen.

The office flirtation between Lucy and Mark was still ongoing but it ebbed and flowed along with Julia's moods. When Julia was good and Mark was content it lessened, when she was bad it crept back. This good spell had seen a toning down of comments from Mark for some time and this blowing hot and cold infuriated Lucy. Tonight out of the constraints of office attire and office protocol she would show him what could be his. Look at that Julia with her shiny hair and her shiny dress. She looked so boring (in a sophisticated way).

Chapter 19

"Could she make it any more obvious that she fancies you?" Julia was laughing. Lucy had just walked away, hips swaying, after talking to them. Talking to Mark only was more accurate, Julia had felt invisible.

"Oh, em. Oh. Really?" Mark was flustered and he caught the look from Julia that registered suspicion. "She's a bit flirty at work but I take no notice." He had managed to regain his equilibrium, he hoped. "Another drink?"

Mark being flirted with at work. Julia tried to imagine what that would be like. He would be tongue-tied and red-faced. Possibly stammering. She was the type though, that Lucy. Squeezed into that dress with her bleached blond hair. Attractive in an obvious way. Too obvious for Mark. Maybe she would bring it up in conversation with him some time and see how he reacted.

But she was aware of it now. Julia's eyes followed Lucy around the room watching for further signs of… Of what? There couldn't be anything going on, Mark was cither at work or at home with her. They had a good sex life again now. There had been a small blip when she had been acting out but things were better now. Maybe she should pay that attention and spice things up a bit.

Her fourth glass of wine was in her hand. Mark, who had been monitoring Julia so carefully recently, couldn't have been counting. Why was he distracted? Was his mind on something else? Or someone else? What had been an enjoyable evening was rapidly being ruined by her overactive imagination. She had never felt jealous of Mark before and wondered why she was feeling that way now.

They caught a taxi home from the party. Mark wasn't one for taking a taxi because of the expense but he wouldn't drink and drive. Julia kicked off her shoes as soon as they got into the house and put the kettle on. "Did you enjoy yourself?" she asked.

"It was ok. The buffet was so so. You could have done much better." A quick cup of coffee and then off to bed where Julia made Mark a very happy man.

In the morning Julia drew the curtains onto a bright crisp day. She was slightly fuzzy headed and opened the back door to get a breath of fresh air. She took a step outside and then strolled across the lawn to the pump. The two cups of water she drank made her feel better and made everything that happened the night before seem clear.

Chapter 20

As she sipped at her water suspicion crept into her mind. How could she have been so blind?

There was definitely something going on with Mark and Lucy. Maybe not going on but whatever it was would have to be nipped in the bud. He wasn't the greatest husband in the world but he was hers and she intended to keep him.

He wasn't the greatest husband in the world. Had she really thought that? Julia had always admired Mark for his quiet reliability. He worked hard, earned a good salary and had been patient with her during her depression. More recently he had shown great stoicism in the face of her more extreme behaviour. The very things that had once seemed so valuable now seemed so stifling. But he was her husband. Till death us do part.

Mark emerged from the shower a soppy grin on his face held over from the activities of the night before. "Tell me about Lucy, the one with the crush on you." Julia had pounced. No easing into the day with a cup of coffee or a cheery 'Good morning'.

"There's nothing to tell."

An hour later Julia had learned that Lucy was 23, still lived at home with her parents, loved dogs and ate cheese sandwiches every day for lunch. The information had been prised from Mark bit by bit. It wasn't much but it was a lot more than there was 'nothing to tell'.

Mark was somewhat flummoxed by this display of jealousy from Julia. Especially as it was so totally unwarranted. He had traded comments with Lucy and enjoyed her attention but that was as far as it was ever going to go. Julia had been joking with him about Lucy at the party (soiree). It was as if something had turned her mild amusement into a festering resentment overnight. These mood swings were becoming a real problem.

After Pilates class the next week Julia and Faith went off to the cafe. "I really don't think you've got anything to worry about." Faith had listened to the story of the party, the dress and the interrogation.

"He knows that she likes dogs. .He knows what she has for lunch every day," Julia complained. It was hardly the most compelling evidence of an affair.

"Look, you're away for Christmas. Take the time to be together and enjoy each other's company. Don't nag him about Lucy or you'll drive him towards her." Sound advice from Faith which would likely be ignored.

Each hour of each day found Julia working herself up about the imagined affair. Some part of her knew it was irrational but the drama it fomented fed something in her. She veered between showing Mark affection and questioning him aggressively about his time at work. He was looking forward to spending Christmas with her family, he never imagined thinking that, so that there would be a human buffer from the constant barrage of Julia's attacks. He had seen her checking the collars of his shirts and rifling through his pockets.

They would be leaving Christmas Eve and heading for Julia's parents Penny and Bob. That evening they would make a visit to Mark's parents Bill and Margaret. Christmas day was back at Penny and Bob's and would see the three sisters and their families in attendance, Kelly and her husband Ed and their twin eight year old boys Liam and Luke and Sarah and her five year old Angus and themselves. They suspected that Angus' father was Scottish (because of his name) but Sarah had never divulged the details. She was so contrary that nobody knew for sure, she could have chosen the name to throw them off the scent.

The family had agreed some time ago that presents were only for the children. A relief for Julia who found it hard to buy for the woman who had everything, Kelly, and the woman who liked nothing, Sarah. If you bought anything for her parents they said they loved it but you never knew if that was true. Young boys were relatively easy to buy for. Something computer related or electronic usually did the trick.

Preparations were made for the journey. The car packed with the boys' presents, a small suitcase and containers of food that Julia had prepared, mince pies, a Christmas cake and a box of homemade sweets which included fudge and chocolate truffles. She also put two litre bottles of her pump water into a backpack with her toiletries. No need for Mark to forage in there. Mark meanwhile had checked the tyre pressures and the oil and had filled up the petrol tank. Cautious as ever, they were only going a hundred miles, thought Julia.

Chapter 21

It was the same every year. Driving to the coast on Christmas Eve had one inevitable consequence. Traffic jams. Mark was not disposed to change even when it made sense, so here they were again. Leaving at the same time and taking the same route. Julia had not attempted to suggest a different start time. It would be like banging one's head against a brick wall.

The nagging of the previous few days and the anticipation of a fraught journey had created a tense atmosphere in the car. Mark tuned the radio to some classic light music channel and after adjusting the mirror, he drove the bloody car every day, they set off. The only way Julia could cope was to feign sleep. Alas her plan was doomed to failure. "Could you pass me a boiled sweet? I need a drink of water. Look an Eddie Stobart lorry. I've never seen so much traffic." Mark managed to pass his comments at regular intervals, denying her any chance of peace and quiet. And they hadn't even got there yet. What further horrors was she going to face from the family?

Two and a half hours later they arrived. At this stage on Christmas Eve it was only Penny and Bob at home. Julia could not have coped with the rest of the family as well after the journey from hell. Into the house, drop stuff off, quick cup of tea back in the car and on to Bill and Margaret's. Why did they bother? Mark's parents always seemed rather put out by visitors and, never particularly communicative, conversation was stilted.

The usual formalities about health, journey and weather were covered as Julia smiled sweetly at Mark's parents. Their modest daughter-in-law was exactly who they would have chosen so they were astonished by her reply to their question asking what she had been doing lately.

"Are you still going to exercise classes?"

"Yes, I've got to keep myself in shape to stop Mark sniffing around the secretaries in his office."

The look on everyone's faces was priceless and Julia revelled in it. The sweet smile was still firmly fixed on her face. Mark's expression was not so pleasant. Margaret struggled to her feet declaring, "Let's have a cup of tea." Julia's comment was deftly ignored by a family well practised in denial. When they left Bill shook Mark's hand and fixed him with an inquisitive look. More communication than they normally managed

Back at Penny and Bob's they had dinner which was some sort of grey casserole. Julia was tired now, thank God, so didn't say much about the food just picking at it wearily. Everyone was having an early night ready to cope with the kids the next day and Penny was putting the turkey on at 5am to make sure it would be cooked properly. It wouldn't be turkey it would be a dried husk.

Chapter 22

At 10am, the designated time of arrival, Kelly and Ed pulled up outside the house and the boys spilled out. It would be another half an hour before Sarah and Angus put in an appearance. Julia had dressed with care that morning. She was wearing a moss green, long sleeved jersey dress which skimmed her toned body. Good old Pilates. Mark was in chinos shirt and jumper (chosen by Julia). He didn't do casual very well.

The containers of food had been held back to today so that all could marvel at Julia's supreme skill. She waited for the presents to be opened and the dust to settle before producing the goods. "Come on, you didn't make these. They look far too good," Kelly was incredulous.

"They're from Marks and Sparks I reckon," Sarah said.

Julia glared at Mark prompting him to action. "Julia did make them. She's become very good at cooking in the last six months."

When the beautifully presented boxes of sweets appeared and it was advised that Julia had made these too looks of amazement were exchanged. "My God, they even taste alright." Bob's comment had everybody laughing.

This was not the triumph that Julia had imagined. She slipped out of the room and went to the bedroom for a drink of water. On the way back she stopped at the kitchen and poured herself a large glass of wine. It was 11.30am. Mark noticed her come back to the lounge, glass in hand, and braced himself for what might come next. Julia and Mark never really talked about their families, there was too much angst involved. Mark dare not say anything to Julia about her drinking in front of the others. It would be a terrible betrayal.

As a way of distracting Julia from her wine when he got her on her own Mark suggested that she offer to help her mother in the kitchen. Julia looked at him as if he were mad. "They have made their feelings about my cooking abundantly clear. Sniggering and making sarcastic comments. They deserve to eat whatever shit my mother serves up to them."

Mark was getting very nervous. "Don't let them get to you. If you show you're annoyed they will have won."

Julia shrugged in acknowledgement of his point. It was a hackneyed comment and she didn't subscribe to it at all.

There was a lull until lunch. The eye of the storm. The cremated turkey was brought to the table with a flourish met by the obligatory oohs and ahs from all but Julia. Sarah had recently decided that she and Angus were vegetarians so a shop bought nut roast was provided for her. Lucky lucky Sarah, thought Julia. She had half a chance of getting through this without raging indigestion. Angus didn't want to be a vegetarian and had grabbed two pigs in blankets to go with his nut roast.

Liam and Luke were turning up their noses at the vegetables. Julia couldn't blame them everything looked like it had been boiled for three days. Ed and Kelly pleaded with their children to eat something healthy and Sarah was trying to flick the offending meat off Angus' plate. Penny and Bob, indulgent grandparents, thought that it would be alright, "Just this once," for Angus to eat meat and that the twins shouldn't be forced to have something they didn't want. Julia stood up, took her wine glass and walked out of the room.

Sadly, it took some 10 minutes before somebody enquired of her whereabouts. Mark had noticed her leave but was afraid of what would happen when she got back. "JULIA!" shrieked Kelly. "It's getting cold."

Julia appeared in the door frame, holding on to it to steady herself, and surveyed the scene. "It doesn't matter if it's getting cold it tastes bloody awful either way."

"Mum's gone to all this effort, sit down and eat. And don't swear in front of the children," Kelly scolded.

Sarah examined Julia. She was different. She was drunk!

"God. Don't you ever get tired of the sound of your own voice Kelly?" Julia was warming to her theme. "Don't swear in front of the brats you mean. They didn't have the manners to say thank you or even feign interest in their presents. Whether they eat their vegetables or not is the least of your troubles," she carried on. "And Sarah, let Angus have some meat for fuck's sake. He's five years old, you don't want him growing into some puny ashen faced hippy like one of your boyfriends. By the way, which one of the dozens of them is his father?"

A strange inertia had swept over Mark. He wanted to move, to stop the carnage, but neither his legs nor his voice would work. Fortunately, Julia noticed that her glass was empty and left the room in search of replenishments. "Does that mean I can have the sausage back?" asked Angus.

Chapter 23

Mark persuaded a now visibly swaying Julia to go for a lie down because she 'looked tired'.

The euphemism fooled nobody. The rest of the meal was subdued but Kelly had fixed Mark with a penetrating glare and declared, "When the kids are playing later we need to have a talk." So after a runny trifle, preferable to the rock hard Christmas pudding, the family summit was convened.

"She was drunk," Sarah said, slightly amused by the notion. Penny and Bob turned to Kelly and asked that she and Ed talk to Mark while they were washing up. So far, so predictable. Mark took a deep breath and then filled them in on Julia's increasingly bizarre behaviour over the last year. He included the drinking, the rudeness, the groundless suspicions that he was having an affair, the lack of ironing but could not bring himself to mention the shoplifting. They had enough to consider.

Sarah could not mask her glee that Julia was rapidly becoming the black sheep of the family. Kelly however was adamant that, "Something must be done." She fetched a pen and paper and began a list for Mark (another list maker). He must be more assertive. He must accompany her to the shops to regulate the purchase of alcohol. He must enlist Julia's friends to keep an eye on her. He must, if all else failed, call in professional help, a doctor or psychologist. It seemed he must deal with this on his own.

Julia stayed in the bedroom until they left the next morning. Mark had brought her some cold ham and turkey in the evening which looked no better under the low lighting of the room. She wasn't embarrassed by what had happened she just couldn't bear speaking to those people again. In fact, she felt a great sense of release at finally having the guts to put her sisters in their place. Her parents hugged her closely before she left the next day, a surprisingly affecting moment.

The car ride home, mercifully shorter than the journey there, was undertaken mostly in silence. Julia knew that once at home Mark would be in full lecture mode. How boring. She had probably peaked too early with the wine but it had been wonderful to get off her chest that which had been festering for all these years. Their faces had been a picture.

Unpacking the car Julia discovered a plate of turkey wrapped in foil which her mother had kindly provided. She dumped it plate and all straight into the bin. Mark made coffee, his standby in awkward situations, and sat opposite Julia at the pine table. Her face said 'come on, let's have it'. Yes, she had been drunk and yes, she had been rude and yes, Mark was cross. He also knew that her family had long been a source of anxiety to Julia. His lecture proceeded along those lines. There was a reason behind her actions but there could be no more excuses. He would give her all the help he could but if necessary they would consult someone else. Julia maintained that her drinking was, generally, under control but the stress of Christmas with all the family crammed into the semidetached house had made her relapse. He could see that couldn't he? Yes, and no.

Once again the next couple of weeks were stressful. Mark watched Julia constantly and Julia tried not to be watched. An invitation to Emily's on New Year's Eve had been declined by Mark much to Julia's annoyance. Apparently she had a terrible cold and they couldn't attend.

At Pilates class in the new year the middles discussed their Christmases. They all had stories about their families' foibles. Emily could not get over the fact that her mother-in-law had bought her a bread maker. She was not disposed to cooking or household chores in general. Why make your own bread when there was a wonderful artisan bakery in the town? "Now I've got to find the cupboard space to store it," she wailed. Zoe's day had been planned with military precision and had, of course, been drama free. She did admit to eating carbs and even dessert. Her admission was made in the tone of someone confessing to a heinous crime.

The stories of imagined slights and minor cooking disasters amused Julia. She had told the story of her nephews' picky eating but had left out her response. She was still trying to ingratiate herself with the crowd again and didn't want to supply them with new evidence of her instability. The word instability had come to mind but then she questioned it. All these incidents had occurred because she was stronger and more determined not because she was unstable.

It was Mark's birthday in January. Julia would make a special meal and get him some nice presents. She was forever seeking forgiveness from someone and it was exhausting. Would there come a point when she just didn't bother anymore?

Chapter 24

Julia had put a lot of thought into what to buy Mark for his birthday. She had decided that she would get him golf lessons. He had always wanted to play, Maurice and Martin did and Alex had mentioned it, and it would also get him out of her hair at the weekends. She hoped to God that he was half decent and kept going once his lessons were over. Mind you Mark was never one to give up on anything and she knew his dogged approach would be applied to the game of golf. She also bought some lingerie for herself which Mark would like. That was another present wasn't it? She hadn't forgotten about Lucy.

Mark had convinced himself that Julia's Christmas antics could be explained away by her family dynamic (he would excuse her one last time) particularly as there had been no drinking binge since. It was his birthday and Julia was preparing a special meal and would give him his present that evening. The menu for the evening was broccoli and stilton soup followed by duck breast with a fig confit and mousse for dessert. Cooking, though still enjoyable, did not fill a void like it used to for Julia. Mark arrived home at 6.20pm as he did every night. Julia made him a cup of tea whilst he changed out of his suit. She would give him his present then they would have dinner. Perfect.

Mark said he was "very pleased" with his golf lessons and he "liked" the designer polo shirt as well. The soup was "tasty" and the duck was "experimental". He did not pass comment on the mousse but he did spend an inordinate amount of time scraping the last of it out of the dish. He was so absorbed that Julia had the chance to sneak another glass of wine. It would never occur to him that he might be the reason she drank.

There had been nothing bad about the evening. Mark had not been ungrateful but Julia was seriously underwhelmed. She was battling her demons. The ones that wanted her to tell Mark a few home truths looked like they were going to win. She didn't need more alcohol, she was fired up enough. "I'm so pleased that you were 'pleased' with your golf lessons. I like that you 'liked' your shirt. The soup was indeed tasty. The duck was experimental. What the fuck does that mean?"

That had come out of left field. Mark had thought they were having a nice evening. "Why are you upset? I thought we were having a nice evening."

"NICE!" Julia left the building.

Another rule change. Mark had never had to be effusive before. Clearly more superlatives were required. He followed Julia to the garden where she had reached the middle of the lawn. "I'm sorry. I've upset the chef. Everything about the meal was wonderful. The presents, well, they were exactly what I would have chosen myself." Too much? Not enough? "Julia I do appreciate what you do. When every meal is great you get a little blasé."

Halfway to the pump Julia was stranded in the middle of the lawn with Mark bleating at her. She'd heard "sorry" and "wonderful" but the words couldn't stop her forward momentum so she carried on. Through the border, round the hedge to the pump. Mark was behind her closing fast but she must have a drink. He peered over the bramble and saw Julia furiously pumping water into a cup then swilling it down.

Chapter 25

So many questions flooded into Mark's brain. The whole scenario of Julia at the hidden pump was perplexing. He had to gather his thoughts and simply said, "Inside, now." Where to start?

"When did you discover that?"

Julia's expression was sullen. "Last April when I started work on the garden." The story gradually unfolded of how Julia had found the pump and had got it working. She had no explanation for why she had chosen not to tell him. There was nothing wrong with the water she claimed. It tasted ok. She had been drinking it for ages and it had not had any bad effect on her.

To Mark the timing of the discovery of the pump, the drinking of the water and Julia's odd behaviour were undoubtedly linked. Julia couldn't see it. "How can water change me for heaven's sake." Mark began to count the ways. Parasites in the water, pollutants such as lead and what about the pesticides sprayed on local farms, they could have got into it. He wanted to do research on the internet but was terrified of what he might find. "I think that you should stop drinking it," he said but after protests from Julia added, "At least until we can get it checked."

Julia felt a sense of panic. What was that thing that people did when they breathed into a paper bag? She needed that. She promised faithfully that she would not drink the water until Mark had looked into testing it. Of course he was at work every day so he wouldn't know that she was breaking her promise. The promise meant nothing to her, it was being found out she worried about.

Plans were forming in Julia's head. She would collect bottles of water while he was out and stash them around the house. If he was ever off work sick, that rarely happened, or was taking some leave she would be able to get to her water. She fleetingly thought about Mark's assertion that the water was affecting her but it made no sense to her. She had changed of her own volition.

It was the next morning that she thought of the book Donna had bought her for Christmas. She hadn't read any of it just scanned the photos. She found the page which had an old picture of the cottage. Knowing where to look meant that she could see the pump in the corner of the photo. She checked the details and found that the picture dated from 1923. It had been there for a long time. If something was wrong with the water the pump wouldn't still be there. It hadn't taken much to set her mind at rest. If the photo hadn't shown anything she would have found some other way to rationalise her feelings.

Chapter 26

At work the next morning Mark marched through the building straight to his office. He was going to research this water thing. He collected paper and pen and switched on his computer.

First, being a conscientious worker, he checked his diary and realised that his day was full of meetings and a site visit. He would look into water testing this evening. He was anxious about the pump, convinced that Julia was somehow being poisoned. It would be a most convenient answer to the problem of his wife.

Lucy sashayed into his room displaying a slight pout. "Don't we say good morning anymore?"

Mark barely looked away from the computer screen. "I'm sorry," he managed. "I'm really really busy." She was still hovering so he looked up and honoured her with a smile. It wasn't her fault that his life was in turmoil and it didn't hurt to keep her sweet.

The water pump problem proved remarkably easy to deal with. Some searches on the internet had revealed that a test kit could be bought that would indicate whether water was safe to drink. After updating his notebook on Julia with the latest aberrations, Christmas and birthday meal, he made some notes about the water and logged the date he placed the online order for the testing kit.

Mark felt more positive now that he had taken action. He reflected on his birthday and felt partly responsible for Julia's meltdown by not showing his appreciation. The more he thought about the golf lessons the more they appealed. He had friends from university but over the years they had dispersed across the country. Golf would allow him to make some new male friends in the area. Julia and work had been Mark's life but he realised they had been too insular. Julia had made new friends and so he needed to as well. When he called, occasionally, at the Green Man he chatted to a couple of the locals but they weren't proper mates.

He booked his first golf lesson for Saturday morning. If he had received the testing kit by then he would do that in the afternoon. During the week he had bought golf shoes, a golf glove and had looked at golf clubs. He would wait and take the professional's advice on which ones to buy. Obviously the clubs would have to not be too expensive. He would make that clear. That Saturday he drove up the long private road to Fernbarrow Golf Club admiring the beautifully kept course and wincing at the thought of how much the annual fees would be. Maybe they did a corporate membership? Anything to save money.

Chapter 27

At the clubhouse reception Mark enquired after the professional and Richard was called. Rich, as he liked to be known, was about 25. There was something wrong about being taught by someone younger than you, thought Mark.

His first lesson had shown Mark how tricky golf was. He had watched the majestic drives of the players on television. In practice, however, keeping your head still, not bending your arms and hitting the ball straight seemed a tall order. By the end of the hour some progress had been made which was encouraging.

Back at the clubhouse he bought Rich and himself a pint and then saw Alex across the room. He went over to chat and Alex introduced him to his friends and already his social circle had increased. One of the people he met was Barry, who he found out through conversation, was Donna from Pilates' husband. "Golf is a life saver mate," Barry said. "I've got four kids at home. I'd be totally round the bend if I couldn't get away now and then." Barry had his own landscape gardening business. Mark thought that he could introduce Barry to some new clients, even industrial estates had some landscaping, so they traded business cards and promised to speak soon. Mark understood that this was called networking and he liked it.

"Thank you Julia, I really enjoyed the golf lesson. I saw Alex there and met Donna's husband Barry." Mark happily chatted on describing his first good shot, how far it went and how straight it flew. Julia smiled but inwardly was thinking what a mistake it had been. She knew immediately that this detailed description of his golf shot would be the first of many. She used woman's innate ability to tune out, she was mentally composing a shopping list, and yet know when to nod and the appropriate exclamations to make.

A package had arrived for Mark the day before. Inside was the water testing kit. He would use it the next day and get this water thing, and then Julia, sorted out. He put it to one side for now and would give it his full attention tomorrow.

Chapter 28

The instructions for the test kit were spread on the table in front of Mark and he was studying them closely. He had seen other people, younger men, casually toss instruction booklets aside and start tinkering with whatever it was they were doing (appalling). It was in his nature to be thorough.

Drinking any water that did not show the correct test results was dangerous to health. Mark pointed to the note on the instructions for Julia to read. There were various parts of the test which would look for parasites, lead content, nitrates, bacteria, chlorine, ph value and hardness. Things had to be measured, timed and compared to charts. He arranged the equipment and gathered a stopwatch and a ruler and a thoroughly cleaned glass in which to gather a sample.

What at first was slightly amusing to Julia was rapidly developing into an irritation. Why didn't he get a clipboard and a lab coat while he was at it? At one point when she walked briskly past the table she created a breeze which moved a sheet of paper and was glared at as a result. If he found something she would never hear the end of it.

Most of the tests yielded instant results but one took 48 hours. A vial had to be kept upright in a warm place. Mark showed Julia the vial, showed her where it would be placed and warned her against moving it. "It must be upright and undisturbed." This was the first test he undertook. Mark filled the vial with pump water to the required level, he checked it with a ruler, and then shook it vigorously as directed for 20 seconds, as timed on the stopwatch. He then carried the vial, upright, to its designated place in the airing cupboard. Lab coat, Julia wouldn't have been surprised to see him in a full hazmat suit.

The next test involved putting test strips into a sample and then waiting for ten minutes. The stopwatch again. The results were shown with little blue lines so reminiscent of those she had longed to see on the pregnancy tests she had taken. The lead and pesticide tests were negative. There were more tests that involved immersing various strips into the sample and seeing what colour they went. The ph was between 6.5 and 8.5 which was fine. The nitrates were below 10ppm (parts per million) and the nitrites were below 1ppm which was acceptable. The chlorine was under 4ppm and the water hardness was less than 50ppm, also correct. "We'll have to wait for 48 hours now to check the vial," Mark said. "But I have read that really the water should be certified as safe so we may have to do that too."

It had been draining observing Mark fastidiously carrying out his tests and now he was proposing more. Julia was rapidly running out of patience and took herself off for a nice soak in the bath in search of relaxation. Over the next 48 hours Mark reminded Julia on a regular basis not to disturb the vial. He even phoned her from work to mention it again. Just before the 48 hours were up Mark arrived at the cottage, having taken time off work, and a countdown to vial time began.

Chapter 29

The liquid in the vial was purple. This meant that the result was negative. No bacteria. This also meant that Julia had not been affected by drinking the water. Mark was depressed. He had envisaged discovering an anomaly, whisking Julia to the doctors for tests and then an antidote being applied. How convenient that would have been. Back to the drawing board. Julia could see Mark was troubled but couldn't quite understand why. The water was good and now she could drink it again, openly. She refrained from rushing to the pump straight away realising that it would be insensitive. A rare moment of considering someone else's feelings.

The next step for Mark was to have further testing carried out by a professional. There must be something he missed. Something that the kit couldn't find. He went back to the internet. He read that local authorities were responsible for regulating private water supplies. If a number of homes used water from wells, springs, boreholes or streams it had to be checked every five years. A supply to a single private dwelling was exempt. A risk assessment could be carried out on request. There was a charge for it but, for once, that was only a fleeting consideration for him.

The next day Mark contacted the local authority. Private water supplies had to be registered but no record for the cottage could be found. They were connected to the mains so maybe that was the reason. Yes, the council would test a sample of the water and carry out a risk assessment. Could they have his credit card details please? The date for the testing was set for a few weeks' time so Julia was still forbidden from drinking the water. Julia continued to drink the water when Mark was out.

The pump had become a fascination for Mark whereas it was an addiction for Julia. At some time a borehole had been drilled to tap underground water and the hand pump put on top. He understood that these pumps were common in the mid-1800s and as the cottage had been built in 1856 it all tied in. He explained these discoveries to Julia who nodded interestedly while deciding what to wear tomorrow.

Mark remembered something Faith had said at their nightmare meal at the Hunter House about Donna being the authority on the history of the village. He would look for Barry when he was at his golf club and arrange to meet up with them. He knew Julia wasn't interested so he didn't include her in his plans. The following Saturday, after golf, Barry was taking the kids to the cinema to see the latest animation. Barry rang Donna and she said she would be very happy to talk to Mark about the village, she craved adult conversation, and he set off for her home.

Chapter 30

Donna lived in an old house in the village. It was larger than the cottage but seemed smaller because it was crammed full of so much stuff. So many coats and shoes in the porch, piles of paper, Barry's work tools and toys everywhere. It was cluttered but had a nice feel. Within minutes he was sat in the kitchen with a cup of tea and a slice of homemade cake. "Right, was there something specific you wanted to know or a general history? Or the scandal?" Donna loved the history of the village, her family had lived there for generations.

Mark laughed, "I guess I want to know about the cottage we live in. Did you know there is a borehole and a pump there?" She didn't but she was not surprised. Many of the farm workers' cottages had them and some of them were still in use.

"You want the scandal then," said Donna. She recounted the legend about the local landowner Henry Hunter and his wayward wife Elizabeth. She had left Henry and moved into the cottage with a farm labourer called John. They had lived there for a few months and then had moved away never to be seen again. "I think this was all covered in the book I bought for Julia for Christmas." What book? thought Mark.

In the 1800s the village had a blacksmith's and a shop which sold food staples as well as cloth, ribbon, lace, hats and shoes. It was also the chemist with soap, patent remedies and elixirs. One of Donna's relatives had made gloves which were sold in the shop. The railway had never reached the village but its advent had brought new goods to the nearest town and then into the store.

When the cottage had been built farming was still labour intensive with mechanisation just emerging. There had been many workers' cottages in and around the village but a lot of them had been pulled down and replaced with newer larger properties. The cottage was a survivor probably because it had been outside of the village and there was room to expand it to modern standards. Donna told Mark what the cottage had been like when she was young and how she had visited her Uncle Sam there.

Dinner that night was a Thai chicken curry and sticky rice. Mark had found the history book on the shelf and had been reading it since he returned from Donna's. The book mentioned that a water source was one of the reasons that the village had been established where it was. It was also surrounded by good farmland. It documented the growth of the village from a small hamlet to a more substantial residential area. There were interesting articles about the effect of the wars on the population with lists of those that served and did not return. There had not been many notable residents but Henry Hunter featured because he had been instrumental in the area's growth.

"At last you've got your head out of that book. I've barely got a word out of you all afternoon. How was golf?" asked Julia.

"You know I think I'm getting better. Rich says we're going to do a lot more putting next week. That book is fascinating; you should read it." Mark was off on village history again. Oh joy. She was half listening as she sipped her wine. Wayward Elizabeth seemed like an interesting person and she wondered what her life had been like.

Chapter 31

Henry Hunter owned a lot of land around the village. He was highly respected by the local community because he was seen as a fair employer paying reasonable wages. He employed many people on his farm some of whom lived in the workers' cottages, which had been built on his orders. In 1858 he had married Elizabeth Foster who was fifteen years younger than him.

Elizabeth had met Henry when he called on her father with whom he did business. They were formally introduced and, after he left, her father extolled his virtues and mentioned, more than once, his wealth. Her first impression of him was that he was distinguished, he still had hair and he was nicely dressed. All in all, a good start. Their courtship followed and after two months of walking out, with a chaperone, church attendance and evenings sat in the parlour, with her whole family around her, they became engaged. Henry had of course sought her father's permission.

They were married in her parish church a month after their engagement was announced. There was some gossip that the marriage had proceeded with indecent haste but the lack of a baby ever appearing quashed that. Henry simply expedited the matter so that he could return to the running of his estate.

The wedding dress that Elizabeth wore was a bit too extravagant for Henry's taste but her parents wanted the best for the eldest daughter. Elizabeth felt like a princess in the ivory silk dress. It was heavily embroidered with wide lace sleeves and flared out from her tiny waist. Under the dress her corset and petticoat weren't so glamorous but gave her the required silhouette. After the wedding ceremony Elizabeth's parents hosted a lunch for the guests at their house before she changed into her travelling outfit and left her childhood home.

It was a big adventure for Elizabeth. She had never left her home county and now she was married and travelling to her grand new house. Henry seemed happy as he informed her of her duties during the carriage journey. She listened at first but as the scenery through the carriage window became unfamiliar she pressed her face up against it eager to view some more of the world. As a married woman she would now have freedoms she had only dreamed about.

Henry noticed Elizabeth's inattention but tolerated it on this occasion. There would be plenty of time to impress upon her the importance of her duties and teach her to meet his needs. She was twenty years old, young enough not to have developed bad habits Henry hoped. He was right. At that time Elizabeth had no bad habits.

A young wife who could be moulded to his liking was a priority for Henry. He was a practical man and a very busy man. The running of his estate took up most of his time. He had approached the problem of finding a wife in his usual unsentimental logical way. He had a friend who had a daughter who was young and attractive. They seemed to get on so that was good enough for him. Why make it any more complicated than that?

Chapter 32

The wedding night was surprising. Henry had expected shy reluctance and a modest submission. Elizabeth had been inquisitive asking many questions. Quite unnecessary thought Henry. One question was "Will this happen every night?" She had sounded rather hopeful.

Elizabeth didn't want to run the household, organise menus or oversee cleaning. She definitely did not want to sit around doing embroidery. She began to think she had left one jail for another. Going to the shop was one thing she did like. It got her out of the house and gave her a chance to browse among the buttons and ribbons and cloth on offer. Henry had an account at the store but there were explicit instructions on what she could and could not buy.

The village also had a blacksmith's and a tavern, which she walked by nervously increasing her speed.

The people of the village deferred to her as the wife of a man of importance. Sometimes she walked up and down the village just to see their exhibitions of respect. Tipped hats, bobbed curtseys and people rushing out of the way so as not to impede her progress. She felt important out of the house but inside, listening to Henry droning on about the farm and lecturing her about her shortcomings, she felt very small.

There was no one in the village, apart from the vicar, who was of a similar social standing to Henry and Elizabeth. In the three months since their wedding, apart from tea with the vicar, they had travelled just once to town for a social engagement. Starved of conversation and in need of female companionship Elizabeth had become friendly with a woman from the village called Molly. She had not told Henry as she knew he would disapprove.

Elizabeth would go to the shop and meet Molly there. Her new friend was a curvy ruddy faced girl with what seemed to be a permanent smile. Molly, who made gloves and sold them to the shop, would then carry Elizabeth's purchases back to the house. They would walk miles out of the way so that they could talk more. It was an education for Elizabeth listening to Molly.

Tales of love affairs, drinking in the local tavern and dancing. There were also tales of large families in small houses, terrible food, cold rooms and threadbare clothes but she didn't take much notice of those.

The dresses she wore, the size of her house and her servants couldn't stop Elizabeth envying Molly. She wanted to dance in the open air and sing a bawdy tune in the tavern while drinking cider. It was just a dream. Henry travelled sometimes on business and she had thought that this may be an opportunity for her to sneak out. Everyone in the village knew her though so she could not be seen without somebody telling her husband. She would have to be content with living vicariously through Molly's stories.

On one of their walks Molly introduced Elizabeth to her beau John. He had looked Elizabeth up and down brazenly and she had felt herself blush. John was a farm worker. He mainly looked after the horses but cared for other animals on the farm. He had a way with animals and Henry valued his services. He was rugged. That was the best description. Certainly not handsome or well spoken.

Molly liked his muscled arms and his higher than average wages.

Elizabeth liked that he wasn't Henry. Molly was her friend. Elizabeth had a husband. These facts were discounted by Elizabeth who had been instantly intrigued by John whom she intended to get to know better.

Small and doll-like with large blue eyes Elizabeth had throughout her life been able to charm her way in or out of most things. When she had teased her sisters or pinched her brother a wide-eyed look at her parents invariably deflected the worst of their anger. This approach had only limited success on Henry. He always seemed reluctant to spend money on things which weren't deemed necessities.

The use of the wide-eyed appeal had lately been employed by Elizabeth in her efforts to get Henry to buy her a small dog. She would then be able to take it for walks and call to see John who acted as the unofficial animal doctor on the farm. Weeks of wheedling had finally paid off when she was presented with a King Charles spaniel puppy whom she named Pip. The dog was so sweet and totally hers. It wasn't hers when it relieved itself all over the house of course.

Each time that Elizabeth had got her own way, from childhood onwards, had made her sense of entitlement grow. She had become convinced of her own infallibility. She had got the dog that she wanted and she would get the man that she wanted. Her parents were not classic Victorian disciplinarians and Henry lectured her rather than scolded her so her behaviour had never been curbed. In some small way she knew that it was wrong but she was quite capable of ignoring her feelings of guilt.

When Elizabeth walked to the shop now Pip accompanied her. As he grew she advised Henry that he needed more exercise so she would be venturing further than the village shop. Henry decided she would be safest walking on his land and suggested some routes she might follow. She tried a route which took her past a cottage which had recently suffered fire damage. One end wall was crumbling and part of the roof missing. Elizabeth casually asked Henry about the cottage which he confirmed was owned by him. It was to be repaired and the water supply reinstated. The original borehole wall had collapsed.

For the last month Elizabeth had been accidentally bumping into John. As a Victorian lady her behaviour was refined and her manners impeccable. She had, however, still managed to convey her interest in John who enjoyed, for the moment, pretending that he hadn't noticed.

Elizabeth knew he was pretending.

Elizabeth had inspected the inside of the cottage on one of her walks. Half of it was sound and dry. A perfect place to meet someone. When John stopped playing games, as she knew he would, this would be where they would meet. The consequences of her actions, pregnancy, discovery or how to extricate herself from the affair if she got bored with it had been given scant thought. She wanted what she wanted.

"Pip is off his food. Please can you take a look at him?" Elizabeth's eyes were extra wide and her sweetest smile in place. How much longer would John keep her waiting? Anticipation had been replaced with frustration. The time had come for her to put her cards on the table.

"Best you come in then." This was a long sentence for John. She stroked his forearm as she told him how she liked to walk to the fire-damaged cottage and would be there tomorrow morning.

Chapter 33

What a revelation. Henry, it now transpired, was very reserved when it came to the bedroom. Elizabeth's initial shock had quickly been replaced by appreciation and enthusiasm for John's methods. So, he didn't say much. That was not a big problem in light of his other skills.

Elizabeth was still meeting Molly at the shop, though not as often now. She had to endure Molly's talk of her trysts with John and had to admit to a certain amount of jealousy. Henry was making her take her duties at home more seriously and she couldn't get away so easily, she explained to Molly. Her friend was so easy to manipulate, there was no challenge to it at all.

A weekly rendezvous at the cottage had been Elizabeth's plan. Once a week wasn't enough for her she decided. Increasing the meetings ran the risk of Henry finding out but it was worth it. The inside of the cottage was now clean with a vase of wild flowers on the kitchen table.

There were bottles of beer and mugs and a bowl for Pip's water. John liked to have a beer afterwards.

Henry had seen a change in Elizabeth. Giving her the dog had made her much happier.

Seeing her return from walking Pip rosy cheeked with a spring in her step was good. She had also made more of an effort with regard to the household too. He was content. How easy it is to keep him happy, thought Elizabeth.

Hubris had been the downfall of many. Elizabeth thought that she was untouchable. One time when she went to the cottage she forgot to take Pip with her but no one seemed to notice.

Even if a member of staff had noticed they wouldn't dare mention it to Henry. John sometimes failed to turn up at the appointed time because of work commitments or animal emergencies.

This was very annoying for Elizabeth. Sitting in a cold cottage for an hour with just a dog for company was unpleasant. The next time she saw John she scolded him and made it clear he had to make a greater effort.

John had been attracted to Elizabeth and attracted to the danger of their meetings. Her increasing demands and her nagging were beginning to make the risks outweigh the benefits.

He was still stringing Molly along. She was a good girl and he did feel bad about betraying her. He also knew that this dalliance wouldn't last forever so he was keeping Molly as a replacement. How do you tell your employer's wife that you didn't want to see her anymore?

You didn't tell her. When John had hinted at his worries about detection Elizabeth had thrown a full tantrum and even threatened him with losing his job. He had only himself to blame. He could not think of a way out of this. He had neither the wit nor imagination. It looked like a good idea to share his problem with someone. His brilliant idea was to tell Molly.

Not completely incapable of artifice John had told Molly that he hoped that they would marry but he had to free himself of Elizabeth first. It had been a terrible mistake he said. It was Elizabeth who had entrapped him. Molly had heard the word marry and had immediately blamed Elizabeth. She was quite capable of ignoring the inconvenient truth that both parties were equally to blame. She thought of Elizabeth still meeting her at the shop and listening to her talk about John knowing that they were carrying on behind her back. She would have to think of a way for John to get out of this predicament. She would also exact some revenge.

Molly had thought the situation through and had come to certain conclusions. Elizabeth was no longer her friend and John could no longer work for Henry Hunter. If he stayed at the farm he would be forever within Elizabeth's reach. He was a master of animal husbandry and he would soon find employment elsewhere. The more she thought about the affair the less she was inclined to blame only Elizabeth. John had capitulated to temptation rather too quickly.

Henry, from time to time, called at the shop, mainly for tobacco. Molly lived near the shop and for the last couple of weeks had been sewing her kid gloves in the window with an eye on the street waiting for Henry to pass. Timing was crucial and at last the stars aligned and he was in the right place at the right time. She grabbed her hat, smoothed her skirts and ran to the shop.

"Good morning Mr Hunter." He looked at Molly with some surprise. He had no idea who this woman blocking his way was. "Good morning." He was always polite. She explained that she was walking out with John and that they intended to marry. He congratulated them.

"We will be looking for a home and I wondered if there were any workers' cottages available?"

There was only one cottage unoccupied. It had been damaged in a fire but was due to be repaired. "Oh," said Molly, "I thought that was being used by someone sir." He asked why she thought that and she explained that she had seen movement in the building. She often walked that way and had seen someone through the window. It was odd though because the only time she had seen them was on a Tuesday morning. It was Tuesday morning. Henry checked his watch and said thank you, he would take a look.

Henry fetched his horse and rode to the cottage. He expected to find a vagrant or maybe children there. He had been vexed at being approached so boldly by Molly but now he was grateful for the information she had supplied. At the cottage he was met by Pip who ran up wagging his tail.

Chapter 34

What was Pip doing here? He marched into the cottage and found John and Elizabeth not quite in the act but certainly in a state of undress. A strange silence hung in the air for several seconds before John mumbled some absurd apology and made to leave. "Stay where you are." Henry was frighteningly calm.

Henry didn't show his outrage, he was a gentleman, he just pronounced judgment on his wife and her lover. Elizabeth had betrayed him and he was bitterly disappointed in her. He had given her a fine home and fine clothes and this was how she repaid him. If she liked this cottage so much she could move there immediately. He would arrange for her things to be brought up later that day.

John had shrunk back into the corner hoping to avoid his master's attention. It didn't work.

"You will live here too," Henry ordered. John had very pleasant quarters by the stables. Lots of room for a single man compared to the large families sharing tiny houses. "I expect you to repair the cottage in your own time on top of your usual duties and from your own pocket. Are there any questions?"

Elizabeth cried. She cried and apologised and begged. Henry was unmoved. He suspected that she would come back home after a few days suitably humbled and he would take a much firmer hand with her in future. This was a worse punishment for her than a beating. She loved the finer things in life and having to do her own cooking, cleaning and washing would be a shock to her system. He thought about taking Pip away with him to hurt her more but what would he do with the thing?

The people of the village may learn of this unorthodox arrangement but they would not dare mention it to Henry or even look at him the wrong way. Such was his power as the main employer in the village. He didn't want to look at Elizabeth at the moment. The sight of her with John would surely leap to his mind. Leaving her at the cottage would therefore punish her and give him time to get over the shock. The idea to have the cottage repaired by John, at his own expense, was a masterstroke. He didn't have to reallocate workers and saved money.

Her first reaction had been shame swiftly followed by fury. Elizabeth couldn't believe that she had been found out. She had been left alone to face Henry while John said nothing. That was the one part of the confrontation that didn't surprise her. The sight of him skulking at the back of the room filled her with contempt. She would stay in Henry's improvised prison for a few days so that he could feel that she had been punished and then go home. Until her return she would make the best of the situation and have a little fun.

John and Elizabeth looked at each other after Henry left. They had never had a real conversation over all the months they had been meeting. Elizabeth took charge. "This is a form of punishment. After a few days I'll be expected to run home with my tail between my legs and then it will all be over." John hoped that was the case. What had made Henry call at the cottage that morning? For a man of little intellect, he took no time suspecting Molly.

They had been instructed to wait at the cottage for their belongings. What was a couple of hours seemed like an eternity. Neither of them had very much to say. On receipt of her trunk Elizabeth began to play house, unpacking her clothes and arranging ornaments. She was surprised to see her jewellery had been sent as well. She found a hiding place for the pouch containing the jewels. After a few days she would go back suitably contrite but it could be fun for a short while.

As soon as he could John escaped from the claustrophobia of the cottage. He sought out Molly and told her what had happened. He examined her reaction. She didn't appear too taken aback that they had been caught but was stunned by Henry's solution to the problem.

Not at all what she had planned.

It could not have gone more wrong than this for Molly. John had flown into a rage accusing her of sending Henry to the cottage. She tearfully confirmed that she had but that it was a way of getting him out of Elizabeth's clutches. She had done it for them. What if he had been dismissed? he asked. What if Henry had a gun with him and shot them? he added for drama. John slapped Molly across the face and told her that she had ruined everything. Molly walked away. She had seen and heard of incidents of men hitting their women. It never happened just once and she didn't intend to become a downtrodden victim like one of them.

Good luck to Elizabeth being exiled to the cottage with him.

Molly should have realised that her supposed friendship with a lady like Elizabeth was a sham. She had been a source of information and amusement for Elizabeth who had betrayed her and lied to her without a second thought. Her tip off to Henry had resulted in an unforeseen outcome but the more she thought about it the more she was relieved that she was rid of John and pleased that Elizabeth was being punished. She had her revenge but it left a bitter taste.

There was only one place for John to go now. He headed for the tavern. The thought of sitting in that falling down cottage with Elizabeth swanning around playing house was too much. She would go home in a couple of days and he would be left making repairs. And with his own money too. He got pretty drunk and went back late. Elizabeth listened to him snore all night and fumed.

It wouldn't be so bad there if she didn't have to walk a mile to fetch water. "If nothing else can you do something about getting a water supply?" That was about the tenth time that day it had been mentioned.

"I'll go and get one of the lads and the drill and stuff." John liked having a reason to get out.

"Don't go to the tavern when you're out. I'll know if you've been, I can smell the place on you." The beer smell could just be detected over the horse smell.

One of John's friends who worked on the farm had told her that Henry was rather pleased with himself concerning his solution. It was now a war of attrition. If Elizabeth could endure this for some time maybe Henry would be begging her to come home. She had been sorely tempted to give in. John hardly ever spoke, drank too much, snored loudly and never seemed to wash. He had even raised his voice to her a few times.

Something about life in the cottage was appealing though. She could walk in the fields barefoot. She didn't have to dress her hair or wear a hat. She let her long hair fly free as she walked or ran around playing with Pip. The place was cold sometimes and a little damp and John wasn't exactly scintillating company but things could have been a lot worse. If only they had a water supply. When the weather got colder she would probably go home. Until then she would enjoy her freedom.

The first slap should have sent Elizabeth straight home. John had been working all day and had then called at the tavern. He arrived at the cottage tired and angry. "I'm digging the bloody thing. We're drilling next week." He was sick of her constant moaning about the water.

He was sick of her. That wasn't good enough; "Next week!" she shrieked and he hit her.

Chapter 35

John was last seen at work a week after the incident. Eventually one of the workers was sent to check on him and he found the cottage empty. Henry went to the cottage on hearing the news and, as advised, there was no sign of either Elizabeth or John and most of their belongings had gone too. Pip came running into the house whimpering with cold and hunger.

"So you've been cast aside as well?" he said to the dog.

Henry was not so pleased with himself now. Elizabeth had chosen John and gone off to start a new life with him. Well good luck to them. He would write to her family, who could share in the disgrace, and contact his solicitor. At least some repairs had been done to the cottage and he hadn't had to pay for them. He realised now that he had chosen his bride in haste. Had he known more about her upbringing and spoken to her more about her hopes and aspirations he might have been able to foresee what was going to happen. He wondered what type of woman to have as his next wife. He wondered whether he would have a next wife at all.

Thank God Henry had only introduced her to one of his friends. Not that he had many friends.

The shame of the situation was dreadful. He had an image to maintain and frequently walked through the village practically daring anyone to look at him the wrong way. There was the inevitable crossing of paths with Molly. They looked at each other and nodded before carrying on. Henry bought a fine pair of gloves from the shop, leaving a tip to be passed on to the maker, "For her fine workmanship."

The village was a riot of gossip about the lovers' disappearance. People did go quiet when Molly was around, poor thing. She was surprised by John and Elizabeth's disappearance.

What a strange pair they made. She would never have thought that they were truly in love.

Molly had emerged from her home in her best hat and dress with her head held high determined to find herself a better, nicer man. Something else would happen soon and the villagers would be talking about that. John and Elizabeth would be forgotten. Nearly a hundred and fifty years later they were still being talked about.

Chapter 36

Mark was a man of logic and reason. So when he found himself discussing the history of the cottage with Julia he was surprised that he considered a malevolent influence lurking there.

"Perhaps that Elizabeth haunts the house. Or John. I wonder if they were happy here?"

"Don't be ridiculous. Anyway they didn't die here did they?" Julia was amazed by Mark's comment.

Mr Science and reason suggesting a ghost. She wondered what reason for her change he would come up with next.

"Donna what have you started?" Julia was having tea and biscuits with the middles after Pilates. "All Mark does is read that book you gave me and talk about the history of the village." She apologised for Mark calling at her home and bending her ear about it. Donna said she was only too happy to talk about the village. It was a mistake to say that, they were now all talking about the history of the area. For once Donna was the centre of attention as she was the acknowledged expert.

The story of the lovers and the cottage was repeated and everyone imagined how romantic it was that Elizabeth had left her stuffy older husband and run away with John.

"Girls liked a bit of rough back then as well," joked Faith. Julia told them about Mark's worry that they were haunted.

"Ooh are there any village ghost stories?" Emily said gleefully. Donna couldn't recall anything but she did wonder about her own home. When she had worn gloves she always put them on the table in the hall and they were never there the next day. She asked Barry and the kids about it and they all swore that they hadn't moved them. Often they appeared on the window seat that looked out over the high street.

The man from the local authority had come to check the water. He had taken samples for analysis and carried out a risk assessment. He had explained to Julia about pesticides and old pipes and corrosion and on and on. Mark asked her about the visit, wanting to know everything he had said. She managed to remember some things but he was irritated by the lack of detail. It would be a couple of weeks before the results from the samples and a report would arrive.

If it had been that important he should have taken time off work and been there himself. Julia was now almost constantly annoyed by Mark's nit-picking. Had he always been such a pedant? Maybe he couldn't leave work because he couldn't bear to be parted from Lucy. She was the only thing haunting Julia. She had no reason to be suspicious. No hint of anything from Mark's behaviour. When she went through his pockets, read his texts and pored over his bank statements nothing could be found. She ignored the facts and continued to believe in Mark's guilt.

Great caution had to be observed by Mark if he talked about work. He had inadvertently mentioned Lucy's name a couple of times and Julia had jumped on it straight away. Her obsession with Lucy was bewildering to him. He had looked at Lucy appreciatively on occasion and sometimes exchanged some banter but it was all pretty harmless. He hoped Julia was more settled now. Her drinking had not been a problem lately and, since his birthday, there had been no fits of temper. In his notebook he had started a new section about Julia's unfounded jealousy.

A trip to the Fox and Hounds in town had been arranged for Thursday after work for Martin's birthday. Mark had to attend but was not looking forward to telling Julia. The usual inquisition about who was going would follow. He would say Lucy was going otherwise it would look like he was trying to hide it. He rehearsed several ways of introducing the subject but he knew that Julia would find fault with whatever he said.

That evening Mark broached the subject with Julia and waited for the fallout. "I don't want you to go. Not with her there."

Julia was adamant. "It's Martin's birthday I have to go. Everyone from the office is going."

Back and forth it went all evening resulting in Julia stomping off to bed without saying goodnight. She quite enjoyed having an excuse to harangue Mark. Seeing his bewildered little face as she swept out of the room was hilarious.

Mark had stuck to his guns and was now standing in the pub with people from the office. He was holding a pint of shandy, he was driving. His first thought was to ensure that he stayed well away from Lucy whilst they were in the pub. If Julia heard any talk of them fraternising, there would be hell to pay. The whole thing was ridiculous. If he avoided Lucy it would be pandering to Julia's insecurities and he had nothing to hide. He approached a group, which included Lucy, and joined the conversation. He kept the talk light-hearted and addressed the whole group so that no one could have any suspicion. He also kept his eye on the time. He followed his shandy with a coke, you couldn't be too careful, and left the pub at 7.30.

His dinner was slapped down in front of him. It was liver, he hated liver. Julia's expression could only be described as murderous. She sat at the table; she had already had dinner, and watched him eat. It took two glasses of water to get through the liver. Bite, chew, gulp. The expression on Julia's face changed as he ate. She liked seeing him suffer. Mark was unnerved by that. At the end he said, "Thank you."

"Did you enjoy that?" Julia asked.

"No I didn't."

As they bickered throughout the evening Mark was relieved that Julia hadn't used the scenario as an excuse to drink. Alcohol would have made a bad situation worse. Mark summoned his self-control and fixed Julia with a hard stare. He explained to her that he was sick to death with her and this Lucy thing. There was absolutely nothing going on. He was not one to put his foot down, that was such an old-fashioned thing for a man to do, but enough was enough. She was not to talk about, or allude to, this imaginary affair with Lucy ever again.

Julia dredged up an apology. For the accusations, not the liver. She had quite liked torturing him with the liver. She went over the particulars in her head and grudgingly admitted that maybe he was innocent. She would keep quiet but maintain her vigil of his bank statements etc. It was a diversion having a (imagined) problem to pick at. It was fun to watch Mark squirm uncomfortably as well. Oh well she would have to find a new pastime. She must get hold of his briefcase at some time and check its contents just in case.

It was Julia's birthday in February so now was a good time for her to rein back lest it affected Mark's present buying. She would have to start dropping hints. She didn't want a practical present, which is what Mark would choose, she wanted something gratuitous. Something big and shiny that she could parade in front of the middles. Past presents had included an electronic personal organiser, for the woman who never went anywhere and numerous cookery books. OK they had come in handy since but at the time she couldn't even boil an egg. His attempts to buy her clothes were even more disastrous. Did he really want her to dress like his mother? Her birthday had been mentioned casually at Pilates. If she didn't get a present from her friends she would be furious.

The Lucy thing, or as it now seemed nothing, had given Julia a problem to pick at. There was a desire in her to have an occupation. Gardening, cooking, drinking and then Lucy had all taken their turn. She was now frantically searching for the latest replacement. She wandered to the garden to replenish her water bottles. The weekend was nearing and Mark would see if she used the pump.

Mark was grateful that the Lucy fiasco had been put to bed. (Not the best choice of words.) Keen not to rock the boat Mark's tactic concerning Julia's birthday was to take her shopping and let her choose. He couldn't risk a faux pas shattering the peace. She had been unhappy with some of his choices. He didn't know why. Julia took him to her favourite designer store, one she hadn't stolen from, and selected a buttery soft, pale blue leather jacket. Mark gulped when he saw the price.

The middles were suitably impressed by Julia's beautiful Jacket. Gently touching the sleeve to feel the quality and praising the lovely colour while wondering how much it had cost.

"Gorgeous," said Zoe. "How much did that cost?"

Chapter 37

From her friends Julia got a basket containing designer hair products, a cashmere scarf, a pair of delicate gold earrings and a bundle of sage. This last item was a joke gift. Donna explained that sage smudging was a way to rid your home of evil spirits. Good God, she thought, don't fuel Mark's ghost fantasy any more. Julia would look up recipes that used sage instead.

Well Julia had got presents and they were ok. The hair products were so predictable. Yes, she had lovely hair but there was more to her than that. Yet she was strangely unsatisfied. Now that the presents and cards had been opened she felt an anti-climax. Her search for fulfilment would carry on. First she and Mark were returning to Le Chaudron for a meal which she was kind of looking forward to.

The restaurant looked shabbier than she remembered. She had refined her tastes and was getting harder and harder to please. Did they wait this long to be served last time they came?

Julia wanted to like it but little things were starting to annoy her. Mark had ordered a bottle of Chablis when they arrived which was nice. It was not sufficiently cold and had to go back. A sense of foreboding hovered over their table. It was an effort but Julia made it through the evening without losing her rag. Her steak was a little overdone, she wanted rare, but a warning look from Mark stopped her. "It's fine," she smiled.

At the end of the meal Mark said he had another surprise for her. Thank God, she wanted more. More presents, more excitement, more attention. He had booked a weekend away in Paris. "We fly from the local airport on a Friday morning and return on Sunday afternoon."

Mark was smiling triumphantly. "We've not been away for so long it will be marvellous. I've been on the internet and worked out an itinerary for us." She did not want a trip away. Julia needed the paper bag again.

There were regulations about flying and carrying liquid. Was it just in hand luggage or was it in all luggage? Transporting her water with her was going to be a problem and she didn't want to be without it. Knowing Mark he won't have paid extra for luggage to go in the hold, so I'm buggered, thought Julia. She couldn't get out of it. What would be her excuse? Think of the shopping just think of the shopping. It didn't work.

"That leather jacket and he's taking you to Paris, lucky girl. Don't forget to thank him properly."

Faith was more excited than she. How could she tell her friend that she didn't want to go because of her pump water? She would sound crazy. Julia was worried that she would sound crazy but she was convinced that she wasn't. The problem was with everybody else.

The date of the trip drew closer and Julia's anxiety grew with each hour that passed. The few days before they left she guzzled cup after cup of water in some desperate way of loading up before they left. She took a bottle with her to the airport so that she could drink right up to the moment they went through security.

133

They arrived and went to the small boutique hotel which was right in the centre of Paris. They deposited their bags in the room and briefly inspected its facilities before Julia was rushed out again by Mark. He produced a typewritten sheet preserved in a clear plastic envelope and told her that they had time to look at the Eiffel Tower and 'do' Notre Dame before their dinner on the Seine cruise. Help me, thought Julia. The city was beautiful but it was hard to appreciate it with Mark checking his watch every five minutes. They were slaves to his schedule.

The afternoon was busy, they pretty much sprinted round Notre Dame, and they rushed back to the hotel with just enough time to change before heading to the boat. Was it the pace that was unsettling Julia? The view from the boat with the landmarks lit up should have been romantic and memorable but by the end of the cruise she was feeling quite light-headed and was longing for it to end. And it wasn't the wine, Mark had made sure of that. She remembered what Faith had said and obliged Mark with the best performance she could muster in bed. He was so thankful after the years of drought any effort was appreciated.

Julia hardly slept at all and the next morning awoke drenched in sweat. Mark was up and showered, checking his itinerary and raring to go. He looked at her and was immediately concerned. She was pallid and her hair was lank and stuck to her face. He began feeling her head and asking her questions. "Are you ok?" The first of many fatuous enquiries. "Have you been sick? Do you feel sick?" There followed a guessing game of what she might need. Did she want a drink, food, a shower, medicine of some sort, a doctor? Julia was going cold turkey.

Having talked Mark out of calling a doctor Julia bravely said she could manage a bit of toast and a glass of water and then see if that helped. It didn't and she begged

Mark to continue with his itinerary. Why should both of them miss out? Julia wasn't feeling well but she had played on it somewhat to avoid another sprint around the sights of Paris. She had always imagined that a trip to Paris would mean slow walks through the Tuileries Gardens and lingering in front of works of art in the Louvre. She did not want to see the city at a fast pace.

Her worst fears had come true. The craving was real and the lack of pump water had made her feel wretched. Another night here and then she would be on her way home. Julia tidied herself up that evening and went downstairs to the hotel restaurant where she and Mark had a meal. She was hungry and needed a drink. She also needed Mark to stop fussing about her.

Mark was effusive in his praise of the food but everything tasted like sawdust to her. She spent another night tossing and turning. Her skin itched and her mind raced and her body sweated. She was in the city of light and she looked absolutely dreadful.

At least when they arrived back at their local airport they didn't have to wait for their luggage, thought Julia, and thankfully they were soon on their way home.

"Shall we call at the supermarket and get some supplies?" Mark innocently asked.

"NO. Get me home."

He looked a bit startled by her response but acknowledged that she was ill and said he would go out after he dropped her off. Once Mark was safely out of the way Julia ran to the pump, took a drink and then fell down and sobbed with relief. She was never going abroad again. She never wanted to leave the cottage again.

The next week the risk assessment from the local authority arrived. Mark sat down at the table with the envelope and removed the report. He was clasping a highlighter pen ready to mark the salient points. Julia put a cup of coffee next to him and left the room. She knew that Mark would be absorbed in it for quite some time.

The report was very detailed with tables of information and data. Mark was determined to look through everything rather than skip to the summary. E Coli, arsenic, manganese and mercury were on the list of substances that may be found. Iron, lead and sodium, so many things that could contaminate water. Selenium, copper and fluoride and much, much more. Reading all those names of all those chemicals was making his head spin and raising his levels of anxiety.

There were comments occasionally from Mark when she refreshed his coffee. When he finally finished reading he came into the living room and slumped into his chair. Julia had to ask what he had found as he didn't volunteer any information. "Well, they check for chemical contamination and there's a whole section on animal waste—"

Julia interrupted him. "There aren't any animals kept near here."

He gave her the 'don't interrupt me' look then resumed. "Pipes are a consideration...." At this point Julia zoned out. A long while later, or so it seemed, Mark stopped talking.

"So in summary there is nothing wrong with the water," Julia had grown impatient.

Mark began talking again and after another long spiel said, "There's nothing wrong with the water."

Julia struggled to keep a straight face. "Would you like to try the water now you know it's safe?" He didn't want to but he couldn't say so now. Julia headed to the garden with a large jug. She returned and poured a large glass of water and handed it to Mark.

"It tastes funny to me," was Mark's comment. Good, thought Julia, it's not for him anyway it's mine.

Chapter 38

The report showed no problem with the water. The home test had shown no problem with the water. Mark was still unhappy about the water. He decided to go through the report again and see if he had missed something or if there were further checks to carry out. After putting down the report he turned to the internet.

Julia was exasperated. "How long is this going to go on?"

Mark looked up, "What?"

She took a deep breath. "This thing about the water."

Mark explained that he was worried about the health risks attached to drinking from the pump.

"Why did you get the bloody tests done if you won't believe them?"

It was a question to which Mark could not give a logical answer. "It's just a feeling," he mumbled.

This man who was a slave to maths and science, who revered facts and data, who was never happier than when faced with a column of figures was doubting a report. Julia's patience had run out. "A feeling. Well I've heard it all now. You're the man who worships at the altar of facts and figures. Just accept it. If it was me questioning a report you would be flinging numbers and details at me."

Mark had to admit everything that Julia said was true. "Ok, you're right." She heard the words but she was on a roll and all the frustrations stacked up over so long were brought up. Julia listed his faults. He was obsessed with detail. He was mean with money. He didn't know how to enjoy himself. Mark said he did but didn't have to rely on alcohol. That didn't help.

"On the trip to Paris, the most romantic city in the world, you had an itinerary so that we could make sure to 'do' the sights. An itinerary in a plastic bloody wallet. Did you have an optimum time for looking at the Mona Lisa to be measured on your sodding stopwatch?"

Ten years they had been married. Julia may have tutted or frowned during that time but Mark had never foreseen a scenario where she would make such an attack on his character. "How long have you felt like this?" he asked.

"Since I stopped sleepwalking through my life. Since I realised that disappointment isn't a natural state." Julia stared at Mark defying him to say any more. Happy that she had got the last word she headed for the garden. This Mark baiting was just too easy.

The comments had been so hurtful. Julia had a right to be frustrated and unhappy about things but there was no need to communicate her problems in this vicious way. And there was no precedent. She had always been so kind to people. Even when people had made insensitive comments regarding their lack of children, Julia's worst nightmare, she had blamed herself for being too fragile. How many times had he heard, "They didn't mean it"?

Mark would make a note of this in his notebook but for now he would clear away the water report and make a cup of tea. They needed to calm down and give each other some space.

He was sure that Julia would apologise later that day and they could get back to normal.

Whatever that was these days. He would accept her apology and then concede that he could be a little uptight and suggest they both resolve to change.

Two days later Mark was still waiting for Julia to show any sign of regret. She seemed quite happy with herself as if their argument had unburdened her. No more unkind comments had been made, he would have to say something if that happened, but she made sure he knew each time she collected water from the pump and drank it.

How glad was Mark now that he had joined the golf club, cost notwithstanding, and he had a refuge from Julia's taunting. He couldn't wait to leave the house on a Saturday morning, whatever the weather, and enjoy some male company.

Chapter 39

At the Fernbarrow club Mark was having another lesson. His progress, predictably, was slow and steady. His copy of the rules of golf was regularly consulted and he had already become a bit of an expert with his golf buddies referring queries to him. Of course there was also golf etiquette. He was an expert on that too. Today he met Alex and Barry in the bar as usual and they swapped stories of their magnificent golfing prowess and occasional howlers. Apart from golf the conversation was mostly about work and other sports. It was with some trepidation that Mark brought up the subject of wives. In particular, their peculiarities.

"What's Julia been up to now?" asked Alex, who had witnessed one of her dramas.

Mark explained, "After 10 years of marriage she has declared a dissatisfaction in the way I do things. Which is exactly the way I've always done things."

Barry laughed. "You're lucky mate, you've had 10 years of peace. I've been nagged since day one."

Alex's only comment was, "Don't let it get to you. She'll get over it."

Barry could see that Mark was truly troubled by Julia's rebuke and when Alex declared he was leaving suggested he and Mark stay for another pint.

Mark confided in Barry that he was relieved that he could put off going home for a bit longer. They bought more drinks and settled at a table. "If you're putting off going home it must be bad," Barry said. Mark had to be careful what he told his friend bearing in mind Donna was in Julia's gang. He described the confrontation to Barry who was sympathetic but unable to offer any helpful advice other than, "Talk to one of her friends. You need a woman's point of view." Barry had shown male solidarity but he could understand some of Julia's criticism. Mark appeared to like the rules more than he liked the actual game of golf and his one pint of shandy each week denoted a man who was loth to part with his money.

The thought of talking to one of Julia's friends did not appeal to Mark. It would make him feel very uncomfortable and, he thought, be a bit of a betrayal. If he got really desperate, he may have to resort to it but he wasn't there yet. He went home determined to weather this latest storm and move on.

The cottage was a mess when Mark got home. Recipe books consulted and abandoned and cups, glasses and plates littered the house. Julia was at the kitchen table with a jug of water and more detritus all around her. The look she gave Mark dared him to make comment. "This place is a pigsty." He had accepted the challenge.

Julia looked somewhat impressed that he had spoken out. "I'll do some cleaning later." Julia did do some cleaning later but it was very half hearted. Mark answering back was interesting.

It seemed that new boundaries were being drawn in the relationship. Julia was pushing for change and testing

Mark's tolerance. He was glad that he had pushed back. Julia was glad that Mark had stood up to her too. How could you have a good argument and let off steam if the other party was so meek? It was healthy to argue she told herself.

At Pilates the middles were keen to hear about Julia's trip to Paris. She told them about the sightseeing she had done and about her bout of illness. They speculated about what had caused it and settled on bad food. Julia knew what the cause was but she didn't share. She did share details of Mark's itinerary and mocked his meticulous planning. "And then he produced the bloody thing and it was in a plastic wallet. I'm surprised it didn't have a label on it. 'Important document, Mark's Itinerary'. I'm surprised it wasn't chained to his wrist."

"At least he took you away and you didn't have to do any organising," Faith noted.

"It was like being on a school trip. He stifled me," sulked Julia.

After the class, over tea and biscuits Claire mentioned their visit to Hunter House. "What visit was this?" Julia asked. While she had been in Paris Claire, Emily, Faith, Zoe and their husbands had gone for a meal. "Did you wait until I was away?" asked Julia, her voice rising.

Zoe informed her that Claire's husband had received a bonus and they got together to celebrate. Faith added that Julia didn't like Hunter House anyway.

There was just a moment when everyone thought that Julia would accept this. "You waited until I was away. Faith told you what happened there when we went so you deliberately planned this without me." She was told not to be paranoid. There would be other times they could all go together. Donna hadn't been able to make it either. She couldn't get a babysitter.

"It doesn't matter that Donna wasn't there. She doesn't count." Julia uttered the hurtful words and didn't care. The others made a collective intake of breath.

Donna spoke up. "What does that mean?"

"Well let's face it love, you're not really in the same league as the rest of us," Julia ploughed on digging herself an ever deeper hole. "Looks I mean, and spending power." Emily and Claire were not giggling and Donna looked close to tears. That was the final straw it appeared. Zoe told Julia off in her usual self-righteous way, pointing out her erratic and hurtful behaviour. Julia laughed in her face. The middles filed away shaking their heads.

Donna was being consoled and reassured by the others as Julia collected her gear and flounced out. The middles conducted an inquest into Julia's actions. She was deeply troubled they decided. She had to be to say such cruel things and not care. There was some debate as to whether they should try to help her but agreed eventually that she was not their responsibility.

Julia drove home replaying the scene in her mind. She hadn't said anything that they hadn't all thought. They were jealous that she had been to Paris and had plotted the meal deliberately to hurt her. They should be apologising to her not trying to make her feel bad.

Donna had nearly cried. She didn't feel guilty about that, she felt powerful.

Zoe had gone along with the decision not to interfere in Julia's life but she was now making plans to help. She had always been capable and she knew that she could sometimes be uncompromising which rubbed people up the wrong way. This attitude would however be an advantage in tackling Julia. She would offer her services to Julia's husband Mark.

"They went behind my back," Julia complained to Mark.

"But you didn't like Hunter House," Mark pointed out.

"That is not the point!" Julia was getting agitated again.

He promised to take her out for a nice meal soon. A better place than Hunter House and then she could tell her friends all about her marvellous evening and make them envious of her. Julia knew that she wouldn't be telling them about that or anything else and the use of the term 'friends' was no longer applicable. She studied Mark, who had made a reasonable offer of a meal out, and decided to give him a break.

Bridges had been well and truly burnt with the middles and Julia took stock of her situation.

Mark was her only friend at this point. She couldn't even count her family as friends any more.

As much as Mark irritated her, and that was a lot, she would have to make the best of it with him. If only he didn't nit-pick and carry on like someone from a bygone era.

Chapter 40

In 1929 the cottage was purchased by Charles for himself and his wife Lucinda. He was thirty years old and his beautiful wife was 23. They had been married for five years but, so far, had not had children.

The cottage was still essentially a two up two down at this stage. A lean to had been added to the side and was used as a laundry area. There was a range in the kitchen which heated the house as well as being used for cooking. Electricity was now supplied to the home as well.

The private lane to the house was rutted and full of potholes. Not ideal for the motor cars of the time.

Charles had joined the army six months before the end of the war when he was eighteen.

His training in the Officer Training Corps took just over four months so he saw very little active service. He had been a second lieutenant and was glad that he had made it to the battlefield before the war ended. He was proud to have served his country and mentioned his service at every available opportunity. On his return he had trained as a solicitor. It was a job that suited his skills as a fastidious organised man.

He was 25 when he met Lucinda who was 18. She lived with her family and had never been out with a man until she met Charles. In fact, she had barely been out alone. She was the youngest of four children and the only girl. Everyone around her was overprotective. Charles was known to her parents through mutual friends and his status as a war hero allowed him to court their precious daughter. Lucinda found his quiet demeanour and impeccable manners charming and was soon convinced she was in love. They married within six months of meeting.

Their wedding took place at a registry office with a small reception afterwards at Charles' parents' home. Lucinda and her mother had made a silk dress which was a V-necked column, slightly flared at the bottom, with capped sleeves. She had her blonde hair waved and had felt like a movie star. The families had sandwiches and cake and there was sherry for the ladies and beer for the men. It was a somewhat paltry spread and Lucinda's parents were embarrassed by the whole occasion. As the bride's parents they had offered to cater the event but Charles had insisted that he would pay. It was definitely a sign of things to come.

Married life was not what Lucinda had expected or hoped for. Initially they had to live in a small flat over a shop. A bathroom, a kitchen area in the main living room, a bedroom and bathroom were all they could afford. She had helped her mother around the house but had no idea she would have to spend so much time doing laundry and cleaning. Then there was shopping and cooking. Charles didn't make life easy either. He liked things to be done in a particular way. He liked things to be done as his mother had done them.

Charles parents were well off in comparison to most families Lucinda knew but they hoarded their money. The rugs on the floor of their house were worn and the curtains faded. Socks were darned and nothing was thrown away until it could no longer be recycled in some way.

Charles' reluctance to spend money had thwarted Lucinda's plans for a home filled with modern furniture and appliances. His parents were already storing old things for them to take to the new house they would have some day.

Once Charles found a new position as a qualified solicitor their circumstances would improve.

That was the theory but Lucinda didn't hold out much hope for a nice spending spree. Her parents would be described as middle class and they were relatively Bohemian compared to Charles' family. Their house was full of noise, three older brothers had ensured that, and her mother's approach to housework was much more laissez faire. Lucinda was ill prepared for the rigours of running a household to Charles' satisfaction.

The main thing missing from her life was romance. Charles had not been overly demonstrative when they were courting but she had hoped that he would feel freer to express himself when they were alone in their own home. Five years later she was still waiting for him to loosen up. Moving to the country would, she hoped, give them a chance to relax and enjoy each other's company. She would try really hard to get the home running smoothly so that he would have less to worry about. If he wasn't so tense all the time life would be so much better.

Lucinda was delighted with her new home in the country. She had lived in a town where everything seemed dirty and clogged with smoke. She felt like she was breathing clean air for the first time. Along with the new house had come a new dog. The King Charles spaniel had been presented to her by Charles with a bow around its neck. Quite a romantic gesture from a man who was not given to displays of emotion. She named the dog Dash. This was the new start that she wanted.

The house had electricity but the water supply came from a borehole in the garden. Charles, though hardly a man keen on new-fangled ideas, had arranged for them to be connected to the regulated mains water supply before they moved in. Caution was his watchword and he did not fancy drinking water which had not been suitably purified.

Lucinda loved the old cottage and thought it a shame to tamper with the water. Having its own supply was part of its charm. When she found the hand pump in the garden which tapped into the borehole which had supplied the house she was rather pleased. She immediately pumped some water. To her it tasted delicious. She suspected that Charles would disapprove of her drinking it so she simply wouldn't tell him.

Life in the country was lovely at first but they were four miles from the village and Lucinda soon felt isolated. She took Dash for long walks in the area around the cottage but rarely saw another soul. Once a week she trekked to the village for supplies and a chat with the ladies who ran the local shop. She didn't know how she would cope if they had a bad winter. She tried to express her concerns to Charles but he took her worries as a personal affront to his choice of the cottage.

She began to long for the small flat they had lived in before. The cottage was much bigger and older, everything took more time. The range had to be cleaned. The stone floors had to be swept and scrubbed. They were at the end of a track so dust and soil were constantly tramped through the house. She seemed to be forever hauling rugs outside to be beaten.

Charles would inspect the home and point out the areas which she had missed, or not done at all. He would often tell her how things had to be done in the army and then make suggestions of how to apply its ethos around their home.

She spent a lot of time in the garden. Too much time Charles would say, she was neglecting her other duties. Lucinda loved being outdoors and had been weeding and planting and planning a vegetable patch. She could get seeds from the village shop and Charles brought more exotic plants back from town in his motor car. Lucinda often stopped at the pump to refresh herself while in the garden. She would sip and then contemplate her life and her situation. She knew that she should be grateful to live in this beautiful place but she couldn't help feeling restless.

Charles liked the remoteness of the cottage. He was happy to be alone with his pretty young wife and he wasn't one for socialising or having people visit. In town both of their families would turn up at the drop of a hat. Lucinda's three large brothers were particularly intimidating. They asked her how Charles was treating her and stared at him as she answered. Lucinda had been only eighteen when they married and Charles was charmed by her naiveté and hoped that she would stay that way. That was one of the reasons he chose to exile them to the cottage.

The garden looked beautiful thanks to Lucinda's efforts and she was now looking for a new project. She had so much energy these days. Dash was exhausted when they came home from their long walks. Charles was a stickler for convention and ritual. Dinner was at seven o'clock every night and it was Tuesday so that meant it was liver and onions. Lucinda toyed with the idea of serving something different but couldn't quite bring herself to shock Charles.

He would be out of sorts for days after a trauma like that. She did feel like throwing caution to the wind though and wondered where that idea came from.

The trouble started when Charles came home one evening and Lucinda wasn't there. His dinner wouldn't be ready on time, was his first thought, and then, where is she?

Lucinda was paddling in the stream having picked wild flowers to put in the house. The sun was shining and Dash was playing in the water and she didn't want to go home into the dark cottage and toil over a hot stove. On arrival at the cottage she saw Charles waiting on the doorstep pointedly looking at his watch. He said nothing as she approached merely returned his watch to his waistcoat pocket and went inside.

Lucinda knew she was in trouble and normally she would have begged his apology but on this day she decided not to. "It's a beautiful day and I wanted to be outside. We should both be outside. It would be fun."

Charles was aghast. Fun instead of dinner. Whatever next? "You have all day to be outdoors. Is it too much to ask that you be home for your husband after he returns from work and have his dinner ready?"

Lucinda laughed. Charles was perplexed.

Chapter 41

Charles was confounded for the rest of the evening. He eventually got his dinner at 7.43 and he was restive all night. At breakfast the next morning, which was on time, Charles lectured Lucinda on her behaviour. He was sure that this was a one off and would be very disappointed if there was a recurrence. Lucinda was contrite but only for appearances. Once Charles left for work she was planning her next adventure.

His home life had been regimented and his parents were cold to their only child. Charles had never considered what he may have missed he simply accepted that his family life was as it should be. He had been rather alarmed on occasion at Lucinda's family home where the volume was always set too high. His wife was a beautiful girl who was very young when they married. He hoped that his example would make her more refined and calmer. Moving to the country was supposed to remove distraction so that she could focus on the home. Lucinda now appeared more distracted than she ever had been before.

He had been too indulgent, he decided. Charles had bought her the dog and encouraged her gardening hobby by bringing her plants from town. There would be no more gifts until she demonstrated a dedication to her work. His parents had been thrifty and he would instil the same principles in Lucinda. He did not want to see his young wife unhappy so if she promised to make more of an effort he may relent.

At school Lucinda had soon learned that she was not academic but she loved art. Surrounded by this glorious countryside she felt compelled to record it. She had a set of watercolours and paper and she filled a bottle of water from the pump. She would use the water both to drink and to mix with her paint. The result of her first attempt showed a green field with trees at the edge and a sprinkling of wildflowers in the foreground.

When Charles returned home that evening she was at home cooking dinner. It was Friday so it was grilled plaice and chipped potatoes. Lucinda excitedly showed Charles her painting which he thought was, "Very nice. Will dinner be on time today?"

She wasn't surprised by his reaction but she had been hopeful for more encouragement. She tried again, "I think I'll do some more painting if you think I'm good enough?"

Charles gave her his full attention. "I am happy for you to pursue this but you must ensure that it doesn't interfere with your household duties."

Lucinda gave a short speech about how she knew she had been lax in her care of the home and she would try much harder in future. Having extracted a promise Charles agreed to invest in some oil paints, linseed oil and canvas for her. Painting was a genteel pastime for a lady so he was happy to encourage it.

The first series of pictures Lucinda produced were landscapes, with the exception of a sketch of Dash. They were pretty colourful pastoral scenes. Charles had finally acknowledged that she had some skill and had chosen two which he had taken to town to be framed. He had selected a painting of the cottage surrounded by colourful flowers and the picture of Dash. As autumn arrived the tone of

Lucinda's paintings changed too. Cloudy, inky skies and bare trees featured. Many showed turbulent skies with very little in the foreground. Had he known about or been interested in art he would have described them as being in the Impressionist style. He tried to be objective but found them dark and disturbing. After studying them he declared them a bit depressing. And there were so many of them.

Things around the house were beginning to slide. Charles had to remind Lucinda to do laundry and the house seemed constantly untidy with paper, paintbrushes and canvas everywhere. Of an evening every conversation was the same. Charles would question her about the chores and whether she had done them. Lucinda would have done very little and would then get cross with his nagging. The meal, the one thing she managed, would be eaten in silence and resentment.

The weekend ran more smoothly because Charles was there to supervise Lucinda. She would look longingly at her paints as she plunged clothes into the washtub or scrubbed the stone floor in the kitchen. In the week Charles was at work and she neglected everything so that she could paint. Her pictures were becoming darker and more abstract. Swirls of dark colour now covered the canvas with barely any discernible features. "Is that a tree?" Charles would ask looking at a vertical smudge on the picture.

She regarded Charles now with irritation and sometimes disdain. He was always lecturing either advising her to do something or how to do it properly. He had exacting standards which Lucinda fell short of more and more often. He also made inane comments about her art. 'Is that a tree?' She could not, would not, even attempt to explain the thoughts behind her pictures. Her whole life had been somewhat charmed. Protected by her family then delivered into the care of Charles, her first and only boyfriend, she had assumed to live happily ever after.

Each day that passed made Lucinda more discontent. She had no one to talk to during the day. Dash didn't count. She couldn't manage to please Charles when it came to running the house. At the weekend instead of spending time relaxing together she was now busier than ever. The only time Charles spoke to her now was when he was ordering her about or complaining about her work. Sometimes, when Charles was at work, she cried out of sheer frustration.

Lucinda did not have the capability to express her sadness verbally but found great release in her painting. She had discussed things with her parents in the past when she wasn't happy and had argued furiously with her brothers. There was something about Charles' demeanour however which made it difficult for her to communicate her dissatisfaction. His rigid bearing and narrow face gave him a permanent look of disapproval. If she started to talk and he wasn't happy with what she was saying he would often stand up. He could then look down on her as he interrupted and belittled her views.

It was a Thursday, braised beef, but there was no braised beef. The kitchen table was strewn with paint as Lucinda slashed at the canvas with a paintbrush. She didn't even look up when Charles entered the room. He collected himself and addressed her. "Lucinda. LUCINDA."

She looked up, annoyed to be interrupted.

"Where is dinner?" Charles asked.

"I'm painting," was her only reply.

Chapter 42

Charles watched Lucinda as she resumed her painting. She seemed to be in some kind of a trance. Finally he had to grab her and shake her to stop the manic daubing. Dinner wasn't ready until 8.03. Charles replaced his watch in his pocket and began the lecture. He was pleased that she had a hobby. This however no longer appeared to be a hobby it was more of an obsession. An obsession that was interfering with the day to day running of the house. She was to cut back on the painting or she would be forbidden from doing it at all.

Another day another disappointment. Charles had labelled Lucinda's art an obsession and had threatened to stop her painting. That would make her misery complete. If she saw him reach into his pocket for that blasted watch one more time. What would she do? As much as he annoyed her she had been conditioned to accept that a husband was right and she was not to answer back or question him. Her frustration would be exorcised in her painting. To be allowed to carry on painting she would have to keep Charles happy.

Friday dinner was served at 7.11, a marked improvement. Charles decided not to quibble about the eleven minutes. Lucinda was dreading the weekend when her husband would be monitoring her every action. She wanted to paint. She needed to paint. It was four o'clock in the morning when Lucinda arose on Saturday. She could then paint for a couple of hours before Charles got up. She checked the clock regularly. She must have Charles' breakfast ready or he may stop her painting.

The painting gear was safely stowed when Charles entered the kitchen. "You're making an early start." Lucinda said that she wanted to catch up on her jobs. She said the words but neither of them was convinced that she meant them. By Sunday evening, despite another early painting session that morning, she was a bundle of nerves. The cake and ham sandwiches they were having for tea, they had eaten a roast lunch, were flung onto the table and Lucinda drummed her fingers as Charles ate. He ate slowly, carefully chewing each mouthful. She could stand no more and she snatched his plate away and threw it into the sink where it smashed. Charles turned a shade of puce and stood up from the table. "Enough is enough Lucinda. I don't know what's got into you. You were such a quiet unassuming woman and now you are petulant and uncooperative." Lucinda was delighted with that description.

Flinging a plate, producing brooding dark pictures, it was hardly a rebellion but to Charles it was extremely distressing. His well-ordered life and his pretty compliant wife were changing before his eyes. If a man couldn't come home to a friendly greeting and a well prepared meal what was the world coming to? Charles had never thought about love. He was fond of Lucinda and glad that he had met her while she was young. She was the right age for him to mould into the perfect wife. Things were now rapidly going wrong.

Charles retired early, he had work the next morning, but Lucinda stayed up to the early hours working on her latest painting. She went to the garden for water from the pump. The cold sweet water seemed to give her inspiration.

She fell into bed exhausted at five o'clock shortly before Charles got up for work. He had to get his own breakfast.

This situation with Lucinda was deeply troubling. Charles contacted his doctor, who arranged to call at the cottage and assess her. Charles paid privately for the doctor so his request was prioritised and he would call that evening. When Doctor Jenkins arrived the kitchen table housed a jumble of painting paraphernalia and Lucinda was engrossed in her work. He managed to get her attention after a couple of attempts and he asked how she felt. She looked puzzled by the question and said she was fine.

The doctor tried a different tactic and asked her about her painting. Lucinda became animated at this point and began a long ranting description of her method. She was experimenting with colour, she preferred a dark palette, and was trying to convey her mood and her surroundings. She was asked to elaborate. "It's about emotion. The joy of life and the tragedy of life." Charles was both embarrassed and confused by his wife's words. He turned to the doctor and they exchanged a meaningful glance.

The gentlemen retired to the living room for a conference. Doctor Jenkins thought that Lucinda was suffering from some sort of mania, probably a woman's problem, which was outside of his remit. He strongly recommended that Charles consult a psychiatrist. The word psychiatrist unnerved him but if it helped Lucinda Charles would make the necessary appointment. The ignominy of Lucinda's condition was Charles' main concern. He didn't want to tell anyone about this. He wouldn't tell either of their families but he had to tell his employer so that he could take time off to accompany Lucinda to the psychiatrist.

Chapter 43

Charles had driven Lucinda to the nearest large town where a psychiatrist practised. She had been reluctant to leave home as she was busy with her painting but had been tempted out by the promise of buying more art supplies. They were now in Doctor Pressman's waiting room and Lucinda was not happy. "Why are we here?" She had asked this question many times and had still not got a satisfactory answer.

She had been tricked into coming to town and was now waiting to see a psychiatrist. Lucinda was completely unaware that anything was wrong with her. Could all this be because she was behind with her chores? It never occurred to her that Charles would object to her painting. It wasn't as if her art was a silly hobby. It was vital to her happiness and wellbeing. She had read about psychiatry and she was afraid of what this doctor would ask and how he would interpret what she would say. She decided to be amenable.

Doctor Pressman seemed a bit too young to Charles. Then again everyone seemed young compared to Charles with his neat moustache and receding hair. Lucinda was perched on the edge of her seat looking at her husband and the doctor in turns. "Do you know why you are here Lucinda?" the doctor asked.

"Because my husband didn't get his dinner on time." Lucinda's tone was that of sweet innocence.

"Why didn't he get his dinner on time?"

"Because I have better things to do than cook his dinner." She still sounded sweet.

"Like painting? Do you think that is a good enough reason?" the doctor suggested. The fuse had been lit.

When Lucinda stopped beating him for trivialising her art the doctor had an indication of the problem. He asked to see her again the following week to start therapy and Lucinda informed him she would not be coming back. She didn't have the time. She left the room. A hasty arrangement was made by Charles for the doctor to visit the cottage. Doctor Pressman thought it would be beneficial for him to see her in her home environment and view some of her pictures.

A lot of Doctor Pressman's patients were women suffering from nervous disorders. He had become interested in psychiatry after seeing his mother suffer with various complaints throughout her life. She had often taken to her bed when her husband, children or life became too much for her to bear. His father had despaired sometimes but had held the family together as best he could. He had set out with the aim of helping men by helping their women.

Lucinda's refusal to have therapy and her attitude to Charles were indications that something was wrong.

This was too much. Lucinda had been tricked into going to see a psychiatrist and there was nothing wrong with her. What was Charles thinking? She knew that she had been distracted by her need to paint but he hadn't even talked to her about it. Lectured her and scolded her but he had never asked for her opinion or given her a right of reply. His response had been to march her off to a doctor and let someone else deal with it. He was a coward.

The doctor called at the cottage the following week. He had been urged to come a day early because of Lucinda's deterioration. She was wearing a dress but no shoes and her normally carefully waved blonde hair was unkempt. She was painting, taking a sip of water, and painting. Lucinda had been distressed by Charles lack of understanding and his decision to refer her to the doctor. She needed to vent her aggression and did it the only way she knew how, through her art. She was not going to stop until she felt better. She had started painting the previous morning and hadn't ceased.

"You say she has been painting for over twenty-four hours now and she hasn't eaten. I think we need to commit her to a mental hospital." Charles had suspected that this would happen but was still disturbed by the notion of his wife being committed. How was this going to affect his reputation? The doctor asked to use the telephone and began making arrangements with the hospital. Charles watched Lucinda carry on painting, oblivious to the doctor's presence.

Doctor Pressman looked at the many paintings scattered around the house. He asked for Charles' help in arranging them in some sort of chronology. They were fascinating. Ranging from the sublime sunny landscapes painted in spring to the ridiculous vicious smears of colour completed lately. The doctor was not an art lover but there was something quite moving about the manic winter pictures. When the atmosphere was calmer he would ask Charles for some of the paintings and would then use them as the basis for a paper on mental illness.

The nearest hospital had a dedicated ward for mental patients and was using the latest methods of treatment. Charles had been reassured by this news imparted to him by Doctor Pressman. Lucinda had arrived at the hospital in a straitjacket. She did not want to go.

Charles was advised to go home and wait a week before he visited. He could not get out of there fast enough. He had signed forms allowing treatments for his wife which he did not wish to contemplate.

The first night in the hospital was terrible. Lucinda shook and had sweats. She called out for help and she sobbed with pain. Her skin itched, her stomach churned and her mind produced visions. The visions were of colour. Swirling colour growing ever darker. They had given her a sedative. The doctors had observed Lucinda's turmoil and prescribed insulin shock therapy.

The next day, weak and confused, Lucinda was taken for her first treatment. An overdose of insulin was injected which caused convulsions. After her treatment she was returned to her room where she was strapped to the bed and her symptoms continued as before. Except now she was terrified as well as being agitated and in pain. Surely Charles didn't know that they were doing this to her? The thought that he did know was the most frightening thought of all.

Chapter 44

Charles had resolved to not think about what may be happening to Lucinda in the hospital. He had work and now he had to shop and cook and do laundry as well. He filled his days and it was only when he went to bed at night that he shuddered at the thought of her treatment. He couldn't afford to be sentimental. The doctors knew best and his wife had needed help. There was a stigma attached to her illness and he wanted her cured quickly and quietly and if that meant shock therapy, so be it.

The next day Lucinda was fed and allowed to sit up in bed but was locked in her room. The horrible feeling of oversensitivity was abating but she felt like she was fighting through a fog. If she could paint something it would help. When a nurse approached she asked to be allowed paint or draw but was told it would not be possible. She sobbed with frustration and longed for some water from the pump.

Each day Lucinda felt a bit better but she was not allowed to draw or paint. It was seen as a manifestation of her psychosis. She still shook sometimes and had the sweats but they were becoming fewer and fewer. She didn't ask for painting materials any more having seen the look exchanged between the staff when she did. It was wrong to ask but she didn't know why.

Anyway the urge to paint was receding with the lessening of her symptoms.

The images of her paintings flashed before Lucinda's eyes and she was perplexed. She could barely remember painting them let alone what they represented to her troubled mind. Her mind must have been troubled otherwise Charles wouldn't have brought her to this awful place. A week after her admittance Charles visited and found Lucinda much calmer. The doctors credited the insulin shock therapy with her recovery. They were pleased with her progress but didn't want her to be released too soon and relapse.

The doctors and Charles were discussing Lucinda as if she were not present. She looked at Charles and knew that he was considering their suggestion of keeping her there. "Charles." she spoke and they all looked at her with some surprise. "I'm feeling much better and don't wish to stay here any longer." The fact that she had spoken without being asked to was a bad move. They had wanted submissive and she hadn't complied.

A decision was made for her by Charles and the doctors. Lucinda would stay another week and then her case would be reviewed. She watched Charles walk away. He had come to visit her but apart from a quick, "How are you?" and patting her hand, his time had been spent discussing her illness. He wished her well almost as an afterthought as he left her room.

Charles was bemused and embarrassed by what was happening. He had been absent from work because of Lucinda's problems and had been obliged to tell his employer. His employer had no doubt told his wife and so the news had spread. The owners of the village shop had enquired after Lucinda's health two days after she was committed. Charles had already bought a national newspaper and was searching the classified advertisements for a new position away from the area.

Keeping Lucinda in the hospital was expedient for Charles. He could barely face the villagers and only went to the shop when absolutely necessary. When he did call there he rushed in and out red-faced. The shame of the situation was more than Charles could bear. He made the decision to put the cottage up for sale. They would have to move to another area. Lucinda was left at the hospital for another two months whilst Charles made arrangements for their relocation.

During her time in hospital Lucinda had sessions with Doctor Pressman who was anxious to uncover the source of her hysteria. She was asked to talk about her feelings and in particular asked to reveal her anger and frustrations. As she talked about her life with her family and then her life with Charles she was forced to admit that at times she found Charles' behaviour stifling. Being trapped at the cottage with no one for company had given her no outlet for her emotions. That was why she needed to paint.

The doctor explained that this was a condition labelled displacement. She was angry with Charles but had not been able to express her dissatisfaction to him. The only way she could vent her aggression was with her violent paintings in dark colours. The red in the pictures, of course, was a substitute for blood. Even her dreams were analysed. She dreamt about painting. Lucinda could see some logic in the doctor's findings and as the days passed she was more accepting of what he said.

The truth was that she had recovered fully after two weeks and every day that Charles kept her there after that time her resentment towards him grew. His ridiculous sense of propriety meant that she was locked away for his convenience. At least the shock therapy had stopped.

165

Lucinda, having regained her faculties was more cautious in front of the doctors. She related that her anger had subsided along with her need to paint. She no longer dreamt of painting.

The hospital was grim to say the least. The main day room was full of women suffering different degrees of incapacity. Some of the women frightened Lucinda. Not because they were violent, although some lost control at times, more because they were so subdued. It was like all hope had left their lives. Was that because they were taking sedatives or would they remain like that when they left this place?

In the hospital the patients passed their time by doing crafts or working in the laundry. Lucinda couldn't even escape housework in there. They were allowed out into a courtyard to take the fresh air and occasionally trips into town were arranged. Lucinda had been outside of the hospital a couple of times but had hated being herded around by the nursing staff. She chose to stay inside when she could. The crafts they were encouraged to do mostly involved needlework. Lucinda also avoided this worried that partaking in any creative pastime may be seen as a relapse in her condition.

Charles told Lucinda that she was being released from hospital, that he had a new job and that they were moving to a new town, in one conversation. Lucinda was cured and desperate to leave so she held her tongue and smiled meekly at these revelations. Later when she found out that nearly all of her paintings had been disposed of she was sad but not surprised.

Doctor Pressman had been the recipient of the paintings. He catalogued them all after he had arranged them in order. He found he didn't need Charles' help to do this as a gradual change of palette and mood could be detected when the paintings were compared. He took them to a symposium on psychiatry and delivered a lecture using them to illustrate the subjects decline.

His peers were fascinated by the painting lady, as the case became known, and he was invited to talk about her on numerous further occasions.

Her sanity had returned but something had changed in Lucinda. She never returned to the cottage. She was sent away to her parents' home to complete her recuperation whilst the move was finalised. Apparently she was suffering from nervous exhaustion. A convenient diagnosis chosen by Charles to lessen his discomfort. He didn't want to use the words mania or mad. The first time she saw their new house was the day they moved in. The naive girl whom Charles had married was gone. Staying on the mental ward of the hospital had made her resilient and had washed away her innocent view of the world. People were troubled. People were sly and conniving. People were cruel. Charles was cruel.

The damage had been done. Charles' betrayal of Lucinda could not have been more complete. Leaving her languishing in the hospital whilst he changed her whole life was unacceptable. She found herself in a position where she still couldn't express herself. Her fear of further incarceration forestalled the words that she longed to say. She no longer had the outlet of her paintings either. If she had resumed her art that might also have been reason enough for Charles to have her committed again. Strangely she had lost the overwhelming need to paint and just thought about it wistfully sometimes.

Lucinda stayed with Charles, serving him his dinner at seven o'clock every weekday evening, for six months. He carried on as if the hospital episode had never occurred. She thought about it every day. Eventually she couldn't look at his neat little moustache and his receding hair for another minute. So she took Dash and left.

Chapter 45

Once again calm had returned to the cottage. Julia made an effort to keep the house more tidy and had engaged Mark in pleasant conversation. She alluded to her problems saying that she didn't always mean what she said. Her filter, as she described it, seemed to be malfunctioning lately and this could possibly cause offence. Part of Julia knew that her conduct was bad but part of her, the increasingly dominant part, was not in the least remorseful. The excuses she had made for her behaviour had been for the benefit of others.

She had not believed a word of them and was surprised she got away with it. Each time she got a pass it emboldened her more. She had pushed the middles too far but it was their fault. Zoe had been waiting for someone to lecture and Emily and Claire were her disciples. Faith had shown no backbone. She should have stood up for Julia, she had been chosen to be her best friend. That was a slight disappointment. Donna didn't matter.

Mark had cottage pie for dinner that evening. This signalled something he was sure. He didn't however have any idea what that could be. It was the following weekend at golf that the extent of Julia's spat with her friends was revealed and now he understood why she was cosying up to him. He was all she had left now that her friends had been driven away. The conversation in the bar with Alex and Barry had been most uncomfortable. Particularly Barry whose wife Donna had been the recipient of the worst of Julia's bile. "I don't think they can all kiss and make up after this," Barry said.

"I agree. I'm so sorry about this," Mark apologised many, many times on Julia's behalf and Barry thanked him acknowledging that he was not to blame and that it would not affect their friendship.

Barry could understand now why Mark had been so worried about Julia. These were not the actions of a normal person. Zoe was blunt and ruffled a few feathers but Julia was cruel.

Donna had been upset but was also worried about Julia. "I think there is something wrong with her and we should have tried to help her," Donna said. "The others had heard enough though and I was outvoted." Barry thanked his lucky stars, not for the first time, that he had met Donna and made her his wife.

It was not something he wanted to do but Mark had to talk to Julia about what happened at Pilates. "Gossiping with the boys were you?" Julia mocked.

"Don't deflect Julia, we need to talk about this. What you said to Donna was unacceptable." The lecture was delivered and Julia tried her best to look penitent. No excuse was forthcoming because she didn't have one.

Mark was alarmed by Julia's lack of remorse. He wondered about her personality change and feared that this new Julia would be the one he would be stuck with. The time was coming when he would have to call in help.

When Zoe called Mark was relieved to have someone to talk to. She offered to talk to Julia and he immediately accepted. The worries about betraying Julia's confidence disappeared with the offer of help and Zoe was apprised of the full range of his wife's misdemeanours. She called at the cottage the next day. Julia was surprised to see Zoe at the door. She begrudgingly invited her in and offered her a cup of tea. She was mystified at first as to why Zoe would visit but all became clear when she opened with, "I've been speaking to Mark." Zoe then pulled some paper from her bag, she had made notes. "Mark is very concerned by your recent behaviour, as am I and your other friends. He has told me about your drinking and I have been unfortunate enough to witness your outbursts."

This was not entirely unexpected. Of all the middles Zoe was the only one with the gumption to confront her. Julia acknowledged that Zoe, in her forthright way, was trying to help. She rather admired that her friend would turn up and offer assistance, especially as she had been the victim of one of her verbal attacks. Zoe took some time listing Julia's failings before she fixed her with one of her stares and said, "How can I help?"

The offer of Zoe's help was not exactly comforting. She would not offer the friendly chat, cup of tea help; she was more likely to have Julia doing push-ups and writing lines. Curiosity got the better of Julia and she decided to indulge her friend to see what she came up with.

"I think I lose my temper too quickly." Julia threw a general comment out to see what response that would elicit. Zoe shocked Julia with her kindness and advice. She confided that much of her bluster was to cover her lack of self-confidence. She was very petite and felt that people didn't take her seriously. She knew that some of her comments were blunt but found it helped her to take the initiative and strike first. What Julia was doing though was different.

The hurtful nature of Julia's personal attacks was what upset everyone. Shout, scream even swear a bit if it helped but avoid being unkind. Julia admitted that this was helpful guidance but it didn't really address what her problem was.

Julia's problem was everyone else and their reactions to her. She didn't need Zoe's help but she didn't think she ought to tell her.

Whatever she said now would be fed back to Mark and she was trying to get on his good side.

Good Julia managed to suppress bad Julia for long enough to say thank you for offering to help and uttered the standard, "You've given me a lot to think about."

On leaving Zoe suggested that Julia give Pilates a rest until the dust had settled and promised to put in a good word for her with the other girls. Julia said a few more thank yous and eased Zoe out of the door. She wasn't that bothered about socialising with the middles at the moment but she did need to keep Mark on side. She would have to come up with a new plan.

More atonement was required. Julia had done cottage pie and she had done a lot of sex too.

She liked the sex. Her splendid idea was another dinner party with Maurice and Martin. She would make Mark happy by helping his career. "I was thinking of having another dinner party for Maurice and Martin and their wives." Julia smiled at Mark pleased with her plan.

Mark felt a strong sense of unease. "I appreciate the offer but I'm not sure it's the best idea to put so much pressure on yourself."

Julia somehow retained her smile and her composure. "I understand what you're saying but I'm good at cooking. Last time was great. I know I can do it again."

This was a bit of a quandary for Mark. Julia obviously wanted to do something positive but she had been prone to fly off the handle lately and that was the last thing he wanted his work colleagues to see. "Ok, but let's keep it simple. I know you can do fancy stuff but the less you have to do the more you can relax and enjoy the evening."

"Beans on toast then," quipped Julia.

How patronising Mark had been. Julia had no intention of keeping it simple. She could picture it now, bringing ever more spectacular dishes to the table to great acclaim. Mark would eat his words then. She would carry out a great deal of research to get the best recipes and the best ingredients. The best wine too of course.

Maybe the evening should have a theme. Italian food or French. She couldn't see Maurice and Martin eating anything too exotic (remember the garlic fear) so she decided against Indian or Chinese. The thought of Moroccan or Vietnamese would make them apoplectic. She savoured that image for a minute before returning to her planning. She fetched a pen and paper. Bloody hell what was it about making lists?

Julia would cook an Italian meal. The last time had been French and she wanted to show her mastery of a different cuisine. She would cook chicken cacciatore for the main course. It was colourful and not too fancy for her guests. Antipasto to start, much like Faith had done at lunch that day but better. Her dessert would be tiramisu, classic and delicious. To make the evening special and set the tone Julia wanted to send invitations through the post. She would need to ask Mark for their addresses. Then she remembered that he had a business contacts folder in his briefcase which she could check herself.

Mark had gone for a shower and this gave Julia a good opportunity to raid his briefcase. She found the folder and she also found a notebook on the front of which was written 'Julia'. She stashed the notebook in a kitchen cupboard with a view to reading this mysterious document at a later stage. Right, Italian wine was her next subject to look into.

172

She picked Barolo for her red wine and Pinot Grigio for her white. She noticed an Italian liqueur called Limoncello which sounded good so she put that on the list of drink to buy too.

On Monday morning Julia poured a cup of coffee and prepared to make a shopping list.

Whilst checking in the cupboards to see what was needed she had come across the 'Julia' notebook. She sat down at the kitchen table and opened it. Julia was absolutely flabbergasted by the contents of this innocuous little book. Printed in Mark's impeccable writing were headings which included drunk, shoplifting, behaviour and even laundry. Under these headings were dates and reports. Comments included such gems as 'no recent evidence' under shoplifting and a petulant 'she shouted at me' under behaviour. She noted that with regards to laundry she had been deemed 'satisfactory'.

What the hell was he thinking? Why had he recorded this information and what was he intending to do with it? She wanted to rip up the book. She screamed with anger at what he had done. Had he discussed this with anyone? Probably his golfing buddies were in on it and she knew he had been speaking to Zoe. This evidence had been gathered and the only reason she could think of for him having done this was that he was going to use it against her in some way.

Her initial idea was to greet Mark on his return from work by thrusting the notebook in his face and demanding an explanation. She was working on the exact wording in her head and she hadn't dismissed the use of physical violence. As the day wore on however she considered different ways of showing her anger. The book was placed back in the cupboard. She would return it to the briefcase when Mark came home from work. Her need for vengeance had quickly become her raison d'etre. She forgot about food shopping and Mark's dinner and focused on her plan.

The best way to get back at Mark was to humiliate him in front of Maurice and Martin. Julia had previously suggested to Mark the Italian themed evening which he thought was ideal. The Mitchells were not keen on spicy food, he said, so this would be a good choice. Now she went back to the recipe books and searched under the words hot and spicy. She smiled to herself happy in her work.

At last she had a new venture to occupy her mind. Since she had been forced to give up the obsession with Lucy, give up talking about it, not thinking about it, she had no outlet for her energy. The restless energy that pestered her when she tried to rest and goaded her to ever more extreme action. It was a love/hate relationship between her and this force. Unable to sleep properly but a strange satisfaction in planning and executing havoc.

As her conduct became more eccentric she had learned to become more cunning. Gone was the Julia who barely knew how to lie. She had amended her plan to something more devious.

Rather than change the menu, Mark would notice that, she would simply add unexpected ingredients to her main course and dessert. The antipasto starter would be left unmolested so that her guests would have a false sense of security. The main course however would contain something to give it a bit of a kick.

Mark arrived home from work and when he went to get changed she slipped the offending notebook back into his briefcase. A cup of tea was waiting for Mark when he entered the kitchen. "You've got the recipe books out again. I thought you'd decided on the menu for the dinner party."

Julia smiled. "I have but I'm checking it all again. I want the evening to be perfect."

Chapter 46

The recipe for chicken cacciatore was on the table before Julia. Mark was at golf so she had time to prepare the food, with her extra additions. She had chicken pieces, peppers, a homemade tomato sauce, red wine and black olives. One chilli was recommended but she had five in front of her. She then reached for the cayenne pepper. This was going to be fun.

"So you're having a dinner party tonight. Isn't that a bit risky with, you know, Julia's moods." Barry had voiced what they were all thinking.

"Believe me it has crossed my mind. After the falling out with her friends I think she's trying to make up for it in some way."

Alex, having previously had a bad Julia experience, wished him luck. Mark, who had been nervous about the evening, was now worrying afresh. A vision of different disasters that could befall the evening flitted through his mind. Most of the disturbing visions involved alcohol. He sipped on his shandy in the bar at the golf club and wished he wasn't driving. He needed something stronger.

Maurice and Ann and Martin and Christine were very much looking forward to the evening.

Ann and Christine had talked about the lovely invitations they had received and to which they had duly replied and discussed the menu which was enclosed. Martin and Maurice were a little perturbed by the foreign unfamiliar names for the dishes but had been assured that there was nothing to worry about. "I specifically told Julia that you didn't like spicy food," Mark told them.

On returning from golf Mark found Julia at work in the kitchen. He lifted a couple of lids off pans but was shooed away. "You'll appreciate it more if you wait to taste it," she teased. She seemed very happy today. Singing some tune as she chopped and stirred and created. She even laughed to herself on occasion. It was nice for Mark to hear that. The worst of his fears were being allayed.

"I told them not to dress up, as you asked," Mark confirmed to Julia. "What am I wearing?" He still hadn't got a clue when it came to clothes.

"I've laid something out for you on the bed." Good old Julia she thought of everything. He hadn't seen any clothes laid out for her. "That was a surprise too," she said.

The table had been laid in a less formal way with a checked red and white tablecloth to emulate a trattoria. Candles were on the table and the lights were turned down.

"You'd better go and get ready they'll be here in a minute," Mark was panicking.

"I'm going now. Let them in and give them a drink and I'll be right down." Julia skipped up the stairs to change. It had been hot in the kitchen so Julia had cooled down with a few glasses of water and then in the last hour she had moved on to wine. Two glasses so far. She had a nice buzz now to go with the frisson of excitement for the night's event.

"They're here," Mark called up the stairs. Julia looked at herself in the mirror. She was pleased with the outfit she had chosen. She waited until they had moved into the living room and then descended the stairs and made her grand entrance.

"Good evening everyone. I'm so glad that you are all here again." Julia's greeting was gushing but nobody really heard her words. They were looking at her dress.

Julia was wearing a tight gold dress which wasn't particularly short but was very low cut. She insisted on hugging all her guests who were frozen rigid with embarrassment at the intimate way she clasped them all close. Mark wondered how her chest was going to stay contained in the dress all evening. Especially when she was going to be leaning over serving the food.

Julia had made a special trip to town to get the dress. It was from a cheap boutique so stealing it had been easy.

Having been told that the dinner was casual Maurice and Martin had donned slacks and blazers whilst Ann and Christine were in skirts and blouses. "Oh." Julia looked at the guests one by one. "I seem to be a bit overdressed. Or underdressed."

"We were told to dress casually," Maurice said defensively.

"Yes, well never mind. Does everybody have a drink?" Julia headed for the kitchen pausing to kiss Mark and grope his behind.

Mark ushered everyone to the table and seated them before heading to the kitchen. "What are you wearing?" he hissed at Julia.

"Don't you like it?" She was smiling.

Mark was feeling very nervous. The smiling scheming Julia was positively terrifying. "Don't mess this up for me," he warned.

Julia delivered large plates of antipasto to the middle of the table and small dishes of olives, pickles and sun dried tomatoes were distributed around. In each instance Julia leaned over the table near Maurice and Martin who cowered away like they were afraid of her touch.

Which they were. Just when they thought the torture was over Julia went round again topping up their drinks. "Dig in everyone." She was having great fun.

They all obeyed the order and helped themselves to food. The conversation turned to what they were eating which the guests agreed was quite lovely. There were lots of questions about what was on offer. The Mitchells weren't very adventurous about food and looked at some of the items with trepidation. Martin kept saying, "Sun dried tomatoes." Julia sat slightly back from the table watching the others eat. She sipped at her wine and anticipated what was yet to come.

The plates were cleared away, more leaning over the table, and Julia informed the party that their main course would arrive shortly. "So while we wait tell me about the office gossip. Mark doesn't tell me anything. Has he got something to hide?" Maurice sat up straight and pronounced that there was no gossip at Mitchell and Mitchell. "Surely there's something about the secretaries, especially that slapper Lucy. Is she still shagging Simon?"

Mark stood up from the table. He was uncertain about what he was going to do but he had to stop this madness. Julia looked at him and smiled. "Oh right we're getting the next course."

"Excuse us we'll be right back with the chicken cacciatore." Another hissed conversation took place in the kitchen. Mark wanted to know what was going on, how much she had drunk.

"Not nearly enough," said Julia as she threw food onto plates.

Chapter 47

Mark took over serving the guests to avoid another flaunting of Julia's breasts. "Tuck in my darlings," Julia declared.

A few seconds later the choking and gasping began. Mark ran round sloshing water into glasses and apologising profusely. He had now reached the end of his tether. "Julia. What on earth have you done to the food?"

She looked suitably surprised and asked, "Is it a tad hot?"

There was a pause and everyone around the table exchanged looks waiting for the row which was sure to follow. Julia stood up and downed the rest of the wine in her glass and then bent low over the table to reach another bottle. After a brief glimpse to check her breasts were still retained she started her tirade.

"This is most certainly going to be another incident to record in your little book isn't it Mark? You know the one? For the enlightenment of our guests, Mark keeps a book in which he makes a note of all my faults. He logs every time I get drunk, when I'm naughty, if I've been shoplifting and even how well I've done the fucking laundry. Better get a new pen for this one." The penny dropped. Julia had found the notebook and was now exacting her revenge.

Her singing and laughing in the kitchen had been in anticipation of his humiliation. He put his head in his hands and hoped that it would all be over soon.

Maurice tried to get up. "SIT DOWN!" screamed Julia. "I haven't finished yet. Has he told you about our private water supply? It's been tested by every Tom, Dick and Harry and they all say it's fine but HE thinks it is driving me crazy. That or the ghosts. He's the one that's fucking mad." Between each sentence Julia took a gulp of wine from the glass which she held in one hand and then topped it up with the bottle which she held in the other. Mark was now on his feet suggesting that the dinner was over and everyone should leave. "What about dessert? I spent hours making that fucking thing." Julia tried to sit down and ended up on the floor with her legs in the air.

There was practically a stampede to the front door. They would phone a taxi and wait outside.

It didn't matter that it was starting to rain. A spare umbrella was thrust at them and they left.

No one said thank you for the lovely evening. Mark returned to find Julia still flat on her back, still holding her glass and laughing uncontrollably. Well at least she's having a good time, he thought.

There would be plenty of time for recriminations tomorrow. Now Mark had to get Julia up off the floor and put her to bed and she wasn't going quietly. "What about the tiramisu?" and once on her feet. "Where have they all gone?" and, "I bought Limoncello, whatever the fuck that is."

Mark was not in the mood for discussions and marched her up the stairs and into the bedroom. "Ooh feeling frisky are we?" was Julia's response.

Having told Julia in no uncertain terms that no, he wasn't feeling frisky and would be sleeping in the spare room, Mark returned to the table and considered the plates of uneaten food and the carnage of the evening. In terms of sabotage she had done a very good job. He took a few things out to the kitchen and started to tidy up. He found the tiramisu in the fridge and cautiously tasted it. It seemed ok so he helped himself to a large portion and sat down and ate. In the morning he would telephone Maurice and Martin and offer his apologies. God knows what damage she had done to his reputation in their eyes. He would also have to have another talk with Julia. A very serious talk. She had crossed the Rubicon.

Maurice and Ann and Martin and Christine had got into a taxi and were now regaining the power of speech after their shock. "I can't believe that is the same charming lady we've met previously," said Ann.

"She must have some very bad problems to act out like that," added Christine.

Further discussion ensued and the general consensus was that she had a drink problem. Maurice and Martin would talk on the telephone the next day; they agreed to discuss whether Mark was really partner material.

So it had been all about his notebook. He tried to put himself in Julia's place and gauge what his reaction would have been. A talk about the find or even an argument to clear the air, but to plan a retribution, over several days, was excessive to say the least. He fetched the book from his briefcase and flicked through it. Maybe he shouldn't have written it all down but everything in it was true. And that was extremely worrying.

There was nothing more to do now other than throw away the chicken cacciatore and stack the dishwasher. At least he could fill the dishwasher properly for maximum efficiency not stick things in randomly like Julia. Having something methodical to concentrate on helped soothe

Mark's frayed nerves. When he went to bed that night, in the spare room, he was mentally exhausted and fell into a fitful sleep.

The door of his bedroom flew open around four o'clock in the morning. Julia strolled in stark naked, threw the quilt back and grasped the waistband of his pyjama bottoms. She tugged furiously at them until they were down by his knees. Talk about a rude awakening.

"What are you doing?" Mark was shocked to say the least.

Julia didn't reply directly to him but addressed his penis, "Come on little Mark, Julia wants to play."

Mark tried to protest, tried to reach for his pyjama bottoms and pull them up but Julia was not to be stopped.

As she lowered her head towards his groin little Mark twitched. A triumphant Julia yelled, "Yay!" as Mark was betrayed by his own body.

Julia climbed on top of Mark and when he was inside her she cried, "YES, Let's go."

Good god thought Mark if she bounces up and down any more vigorously she'll damage my spine. His spine was forgotten when Julia started screaming her encouragement, "Oh yes, let's fuck."

Mark was horrified and his horror reached little Mark who wilted in the face of Julia's vulgarity.

"Bloody hell Mark, just when it was getting good." Julia climbed off of him and stared at a cowering little Mark. "Any hope of a revival?" she said hopefully.

"None whatsoever." Mark finally managed to get his pyjama bottoms back in place, his dignity was still absent. "Go back to bed, now."

Julia shrugged and exited the room. "Your loss," she called out.

There was no chance of any further sleep. Mark stared at the ceiling traumatised by the encounter. He made a mental list, he didn't think his legs would carry him anywhere to get pen and paper, of the subjects he needed to cover in his talk with Julia the next day. He had been in denial about her behaviour for too long. The notebook may have been the trigger for her latest aberration but it had also clearly shown her deterioration.

Mark had hoped Zoe's intervention would have stopped things like this happening. He hadn't taken into account that Julia would find the note book and overreact. It was time to call in the big guns. He resolved to telephone Julia's sister Kelly the next morning and reveal the true extent of their problems. Kelly had given him a list of things to do and suggestions but now he needed more practical help. Mark turned recent events over and over in his mind as he waited for the morning to come.

Chapter 48

Julia was in the kitchen making coffee the next morning when Mark came down stairs. He walked into the room with a suitably censorious look on his face. Julia looked at him smiled and asked, "Coffee?"

"Yes I'll have some coffee and then we'll have a talk about last night."

Mark watched Julia busy herself around the kitchen. She appeared quite chipper and there was not a trace of embarrassment or chagrin to be seen.

Coffee in hand Mark retreated to the living room and made the call to Kelly. He hoped that a two-person intervention would help him to tackle Julia's problems. Kelly listened with increasing alarm to the catalogue of Julia's misdemeanours. Shy, meek obedient Julia who now got drunk and swore at people. Who alienated friends with her rude comments and obsessed about Mark having an affair. Then there was the shoplifting. Kelly was a capable woman, a decision maker and go getter but now she hesitated.

Kelly had a husband and two young boys who were always her first consideration but this was an emergency. She told Mark that she had arrangements to make and then she would come straight away. Thirty minutes later she was in the car starting the hundred mile journey from the coast.

She had phoned her parents and enlisted their help with the boys and explained that Julia wasn't well and Mark needed her assistance. Bob and Penny had not been told what the ailment was specifically but they thought it would be connected to what happened at Christmas. For Kelly to dash off their need must be urgent.

Bob and Penny were worried about their middle daughter. She had always been the easy one. Kelly rarely needed them now, she was so competent. Sarah would need looking after for life, she was so irresponsible. Neither of them had caused trouble in the way Julia now seemed to be doing. Drinking, swearing and being rude. It was terrible to think that they may have done something to cause this behaviour.

Mark couldn't wait for Kelly to arrive so he called Julia into the room and asked her to sit down. She was holding a glass of water as she nestled into an armchair ready for her dressing down. Mark didn't shout or raise his voice at all. He was crestfallen as he talked about the possible ramifications of last night on his career. How he worked hard to buy her what she needed and keep them in comfort. The love he still felt for her and the sacrifices he would make to help her get over whatever this was. It would help if she could explain to him what had driven her to act so badly recently and hurt him so deeply.

As she sipped on her water Julia studied Mark. He looked pathetic sat there moaning about her. She had been walking a fine line between keeping him happy and doing what she wanted. The time had come, she decided, to stop appeasing him and everybody else for that matter. He had stopped talking so this must be the bit where she apologised and begged his forgiveness. Not this time.

Julia explained to Mark that she knew she had disappointed him and that her behaviour had been erratic. The notebook incident had pushed her over the edge.

Reading all that criticism so neatly laid out had been too much. Perhaps she should have spoken to him about it rather than take such drastic action but she hadn't. She had done what her gut told her to do. An awakening to her true self had occurred and she could not deny it to please others. The actions she took felt right and she would not be apologising or changing. Poor Mark, she thought, he looks like he's going to cry. Mark pulled himself together stood up and left the room with as much dignity as he could muster. Julia watched him leave, wimp, she thought.

She did not know that Mark had called for backup.

It was twelve o'clock when Kelly arrived. Julia heard the car and looked out of the window.

"What's she doing here?" she growled.

"I'm inviting a second opinion," Mark said pompously.

The bastard, thought Julia, sending for a member of her family. A smart move. Mark opened the door and Kelly came in and inspected Julia. The stare which had so intimidated her throughout her childhood had lost a lot of its power but still unnerved her momentarily.

Whilst Julia was sat there listening Mark recounted their earlier conversation to Kelly. There was no visible reaction from Kelly she simply nodded and asked Mark to leave her and Julia alone. The appealing to her better nature approach had not worked so Kelly was going to play hardball. "You stupid idiot," was how Kelly started. There followed a list of reasons why Julia should be grateful for what she had and should not bite the hand that was feeding her. Was she trying to drive Mark away? Did she want a divorce? The consequences of that scenario were then laid out for her. No monthly allowance, she would have to get a job. That meant all the clothes and luxuries she enjoyed would disappear and where would she live? They would have to sell the cottage.

The coup de grace had been applied. Well played Kelly. Julia would have to back down, again. There was no way she could have her cake and eat it. The cottage was everything and she couldn't risk its loss. Julia thanked Kelly for her insight and advised that she had a lot to think about. She would go and get some fresh air. Kelly let her go but cautioned that the reasons why she had behaved badly would have to be examined in due course.

Chapter 49

Of course Julia was just being bloody minded by insisting on some fresh air. She knew that they had won and she would be a good little girl once more. It was getting harder and harder to do. Bad Julia was more dominant with every day that passed. She went back inside and made them all a cup of tea. It was time for her mea culpa. She didn't revert to tears again, that would not work on Mark and definitely not on Kelly. She went for the hurt by Mark's notebook angle and acknowledged that it could have been dealt with in a better way. People kept asking what was wrong with her but she had no satisfactory answer. There had been a change and she was struggling to find a balance.

Unfortunately, this was not enough to placate Kelly or Mark. Between Kelly's need for order and Mark's need for a logical explanation Julia's statement that there had been a change was not sufficient. Many theories were posited that afternoon including Julia finally accepting that she would be childless to her lack of a job and therefore lack of direction. Even the water pump was raised once more but Kelly couldn't rationalise that. Most of the debate went on around Julia who at one point left the table went to the pump and returned without either of them seeming to notice.

The conclusion was that an expert of some sort was required. An accompanied visit to the doctor's to start with and then, if necessary, a referral to someone else. Julia agreed to this course of action. She had little choice. She quite fancied a bit of therapy. Being shut in a room and encouraged to talk about yourself was somewhat appealing. Before seeing the doctor she had one more confession to make. "I should have told you sooner, but I stopped taking the antidepressants ages ago." Exasperated sighs met that revelation.

Kelly would stay overnight and go home in the morning. The changing of sheets and preparations for dinner gave them all a diversion. Julia made an effort to cook a nice meal and Kelly said how much she had enjoyed it. In the morning Kelly stood over Julia as she called the doctor's and made an appointment. Promises were made to keep in touch more regularly and for Julia to call Kelly if there was any more trouble.

Back at home Kelly told her parents the reason for her rush to Julia and Mark. The details were difficult for them to hear. "She's been shoplifting?" Penny was stunned by that fact.

"What should we do?" asked Bob.

"Phone her each week as usual, let her know you're there if she needs anything." This was Kelly's recommendation. Her parents were likely to go into mollycoddling overload and that could be counterproductive so she had stopped them from rushing to the cottage for a visit.

Mark had been reluctant to go to work on the Monday. He would have to face Maurice and Martin and he would have to leave Julia alone. Kelly would be there first thing but then she had to go home to her own family. At the office Mark went straight to Maurice and asked for a private chat. He apologised afresh and profusely for Julia's behaviour. Maurice confessed that he and Martin had discussed the events of the weekend at length and, with the counsel of their wives, concluded that Mark could not be held responsible for his wife's actions.

Furthermore, as Julia was obviously having difficulties, they would support him where they could. As long as it didn't affect his work.

He could have done without the pious tone of the meeting but Mark was grateful that this part of the dilemma was behind him. The next part, Julia, would be much more challenging to sort out. He phoned home and Julia assured him that a doctor's appointment had been made and yes it was in the evening so that he could go too. Now all he had to do was figure out what he was going to tell the doctor.

Chapter 50

Both Julia and Mark had visited Doctor Young when they first arrived in the village but had not seen him since. They had been given a basic physical and a brief discussion of their medical histories had taken place. It was a small practice and the doctor, who was in his sixties, liked to get to know his patients.

Mark started by telling the doctor about Julia's previous diagnosis of depression and how she had now developed mood swings which resulted in outlandish behaviour of which he never knew she was capable. Doctor Young looked at Julia. "Mark is doing all the talking, now I want to hear from you." She was sorely tempted to tell him that she was there under duress and Mark was making it all up.

She sighed, "I'm afraid that everything he's said is true. I've upset people, made an exhibition of myself and generally been bad. Don't ask me why because I don't know."

A list of other symptoms was explored. Was she eating properly? Yes. Was she sleeping properly? No. Did she have headaches? Only hangovers. Was she lacking in energy? No. Did she ever feel suicidal? No. What about her libido? Nothing wrong with that. Mark squirmed in his seat at that point.

"Given your history of depression in the past it would seem that you are having manic episodes. The dramatic swing between good and bad behaviour are the highs and lows associated with bipolar disorder." The doctor prescribed some pills, talked about the benefits of exercise and sleep and mentioned talking therapies as a possibility if the drugs didn't work.

Mark told him that they had private health insurance and he was immediately given the details of some therapists.

Bipolar disorder. Julia was secretly thrilled to have a disorder. For her it was a get out of jail free card. Already she was planning a return to Pilates. She would tell someone, yes Zoe, that she had been advised to take exercise by the doctor. What's wrong? She would ask. I've got bipolar disorder she would admit bravely. Zoe had been the one to reach out to her and now she would facilitate her way back into the Pilates fold.

The next Tuesday at Pilates she set up next to Zoe as she used to do in the hall. "I won't intrude on any of you," she said quietly to Zoe. "But my doctor says exercise will help me so that's why I'm here."

"What's wrong?" Zoe asked on cue.

Eyes cast down, nervous twiddling of fingers. "I've got bipolar disorder." And walk away.

The grapevine kicked in and at tea and biscuits afterwards the middles approached to sympathise with Julia and offer their apologies for not being there for her. Faith was last to talk saying she felt worst as she had been her closest friend and she should not have given up on her so soon. Julia looked miserable and then grateful in the appropriate places. Inside she was revelling in her status as needy friend.

Zoe pulled Julia aside as they left and asked for a fuller update about her health. Julia adopted the appropriately despondent demeanour as she talked about having depression in the past and how her mood swings were indicative of bipolar disorder. Zoe was pleased that Julia had sought professional help and offered her further assistance should she need it. Julia managed a weak smile as Zoe left which rapidly turned into a sneer. There was no way she would ask for her help. Interfering old cow.

He didn't know it yet, but Mark had fed the monster not killed it. Had Julia's problem really been bipolar disorder she would have been relieved by her diagnosis knowing that she was going to get help. That was not how she felt. She took her tablets more as an experiment to see if they did anything and occasionally moped about the house in her dressing gown for effect. In reality she was having a great time. Say what you want, do what you want, blame it on bipolar disorder.

Julia was looking forward to her first talking therapy session. She arrived and Stella, her therapist, came out to meet her. Stella was not what Julia had expected. She had imagined a new age type with a big cardigan and a softly spoken voice. What she got was a glamorous woman in her fifties whose outfit, a well-tailored suit, and manner said all business. After the preliminary details were taken the session started.

"Tell me about the difficulties you've been experiencing," Stella prompted. Julia didn't really think she had been experiencing any difficulties. Especially since the bipolar diagnosis allowed her to get away with so much but she thought she'd better play the game. Julia talked about her mood swings and her bad behaviour and threw in the drinking for good measure.

"So what would you like to work on?" Stella asked.

Julia looked blank.

"What would you like to change?" Stella tried.

The session was not as much fun as Julia thought it was going to be. She didn't want to change anything about herself but now she had to come up with something. "Impulse control."

Julia was quite pleased with herself for coming up with that one. "Explain what you mean?" Stella probed. Bloody hell, thought Julia, I should have said I had communication problems and then I could have sat here in silence for the rest of the hour.

Most of the next hour was filled with Julia rambling about hurting people, her friends, family and Mark and having to atone for it later. Stella asked the odd question but mainly Julia talked. At the end she was exhausted from having to say what she thought Stella wanted to hear rather than what she really felt. If she did this too often she would give the game away.

When she got home she would do a bit of research into bipolar disorder in preparation for the next session.

Chapter 51

The therapy sessions had become a challenge for Julia who felt the need to convince Stella that she was indeed bipolar. With the research under her belt subsequent topics covered by Julia had included her lack of sleep, the days when she had no energy (she always had energy) and her low self-esteem. She had even been able to squeeze out a few tears when appropriate. Stella listened nodded and asked her questions. "How did you feel about hurting Mark?" and "You thought Kelly was interfering, not helping then?" Julia hated the questions.

Stella had listened to Julia on the last three visits. After the first time she had begun to doubt that Julia had bipolar disorder. By the third visit she was pretty sure. If anything Julia appeared to be a sociopath. The only time she showed any animation was when she described the awful things she had said and done. She went through the motions of saying how bad she felt afterwards simply because that was what she was expected to say.

Depression and depressive disorders were Stella's areas of expertise so she felt that Julia should be referred to a different therapist. She wrote to Doctor Young advising him of her opinion that Julia was not suffering from bipolar disorder but was in fact showing sociopathic tendencies. In the circumstances she thought it best that a psychotherapist specialising in this area would be more appropriate. She would tell Julia at their next session of her decision.

When the next session arrived Julia was already 'over it' in the vernacular. Stella explained her conclusions that Julia was not bipolar but exhibiting sociopathic behaviour and recommended that she see someone who was an expert in that disorder. Julia listened and became more and more infuriated. She had been found out and she didn't like it. Stella explained what a sociopath was and Julia had to admit it was her to a T.

The names of the suggested psychotherapists were deposited in a bin down the road. She had done with therapy. Mark would be none the wiser, she would pretend to keep going for the next few weeks. Happily, all this was confidential so she would keep the bipolar tag as it suited her better than being called a sociopath. Doctor Young telephoned Julia to say he had received a letter from Stella and asking her if she had made alternative arrangements. She told him that she had and thanked him for his phone call. Thank God he had phoned when Mark was at work or there would have been all sorts of questions.

A new name to apply to herself, sociopath. Julia had investigated on the internet what this meant and found it all rather fascinating. The definition was a person who shows antisocial, sometimes criminal, behaviour with no social conscience or sense of responsibility. She had read somewhere that there was disagreement over whether therapy worked for this problem so it backed up her decision to quit.

"How's it going with Stella?" Mark asked.

"She thinks I'm making good progress so I won't need to go for much longer. Of course I can start again if I need to." Julia had seen Mark's worried look after the first sentence so tagged a bit on to reassure him. Therapy done and dusted.

The middles were interested in Julia's therapy too. At first Julia had enjoyed telling them about her conversations with Stella and how she bared her soul and cried about her past behaviour.

Now that she wasn't going any more she changed tactics and told them how the therapy was in a new phase and it was now too personal to talk about. Lying was also one of the traits of a sociopath.

Julia was getting bored with Pilates class. She liked being at home so going every week was becoming a chore. She saw her friends but they were all annoying in their various ways. Zoe was still bossy and Emily and Claire were like silly teenagers. Faith was a traitor. Some weeks she had to bite her lip to stop herself saying what she was thinking. It was only a matter of time before she lost it.

All through the class Julia's mind had been wandering. Zoe had noticed and kept telling her off. "You're not doing it properly. In fact, you're not even trying." Emily and Claire were giggling as usual. That was the final comment from Zoe that Julia was prepared to tolerate. There were only five minutes to the end of class but that was five minutes too long for her. She got to her feet gathered her belongings and walked out of the hall. She was helping herself to another biscuit when the middles arrived.

"What was that all about?" asked Zoe.

"I just couldn't stand the sound of your nagging voice for another second," Julia said turning to look at Zoe with a challenging stare. The clones giggled. Julia wheeled around to look at them. "Right on cue. Giggling again. Did you know that I call you two the clones? Matching hair, matching clothes and matching stupidity."

Zoe had heard enough. "We know about your bipolar disorder, you tell us all the time, but it doesn't give you carte blanche to insult people."

There was an uncomfortable pause as Julia and Zoe squared up to each other. "Thank you Zoe for being so understanding of my problems and thank you to the rest of you for backing me up. Especially you Faith, my best friend, thank you for leaping to my defence." Julia turned to look at Donna who winced as she awaited her turn. "Who would have thought that you would be the least annoying of them all?"

There was a collective sigh of relief when Julia picked up her bag at that point and left. Faith frowned and picked up her bag. "I suppose I'd better go after her."

Zoe caught hold of her arm to stop her and Faith didn't protest. They adjourned to the cafe to discuss the morning's events. Zoe, of course, was the most vociferous with the others mostly agreeing with her assessment. She had tried to help but this was the last straw. Julia was using her bipolar disorder as an excuse to behave badly. Donna even wondered if Julia really had the disorder at all.

Chapter 52

Faith received a phone call that evening from Julia who said, "I'm having a bad day," in mitigation. She then wanted to know what had been said about her after she left. Julia was expecting expressions of regret about how they had been too harsh on their beleaguered friend.

Faith, however, told her the truth. "Everyone has lost patience with you Julia. Including me. You can't keep insulting and hurting people and then expect them to forgive you. Don't give me the bipolar thing either, it doesn't work anymore."

A red mist descended on Julia.

"Well fuck you and the rest of those heartless bitches…" The line went dead.

So no more Pilates then. Julia wouldn't tell Mark. She must remember to talk about it when he came home on Tuesday evenings to keep up the pretence. This secret was not so easy to keep. At the golf club Mark headed to the bar to meet Alex and Barry. They greeted him with firm handshakes and pats on the back like there had been a bereavement. He looked at them with a bewildered expression. "We heard from the wives about Julia's relapse. They've tried to be supportive but they just can't do it anymore." Alex said the words and watched Mark's face. He didn't know what they were talking about.

The gory details of the latest outburst were relayed to Mark by his friends. He had to sit down as he listened to the insults she had hurled at all of them bar Donna. "Sorry mate," said Barry.

"The girls think she's using this bipolar thing as an excuse." Mark was beginning to think she was too. "Look. I know your life can't be easy right now so if you need to talk give us a ring and we'll meet up at The Green Man or something." Barry made the offer and Alex said he was in as well.

Mark returned home and told Julia he was going for a bath. He couldn't talk to her straight away he was too angry. She had upset everyone again and hadn't even hinted that there had been a falling out. What else was she hiding from him? Julia sensed that something was wrong. Those bitches had been telling their husbands about her and now they had told Mark.

He was bound to confront her about it. What could she do to get out of this one?

When Mark came downstairs Julia was sat at the kitchen table with a glass of water and her antidepressant tablets scattered in front of her. "Julia, no." Mark ran across the room. "How many have you taken?"

She looked up at him. "I haven't taken any. I was thinking about it but the truth is I don't want to die. I can't stop hurting people, you and the girls at Pilates, and I think it would be easier if I wasn't around. I really don't want to die though."

Mark sank into a chair and took hold of her hand. "We'll sort this out. I'll give you all the help you need. I thought you said you were making progress with the therapy?" Mark asked anxiously.

202

"I thought I was but it's an ongoing process. I'll tell Stella what's happened and she will help I'm sure. She's very good." Julia let a hint of hopefulness enter her voice and grimaced in imitation of a smile.

"Perhaps I should come with you next time?" Mark suggested.

"The sessions are meant to be one on one but I will ask Stella if you can come next time I see her. Thank you very much for the offer I really appreciate it." Julia was a very proficient liar by now.

The following week she would tell him how Stella had said no to the idea.

When he was back at work Mark made a phone call to Kelly. He had phoned her with news of the bipolar disorder diagnosis and had promised to keep her updated with any developments.

He started with Julia's latest eruption and then told her about the pills. Kelly was ready to drop everything and come for another visit but Mark forestalled her. He explained that, loth as he was to admit it, Julia had engineered the whole situation to gain sympathy. She had pushed her friends away again and tried to hide it from him. Once she realised he had found out she had pulled her pills stunt.

Kelly was staggered by the revelation. "Are you sure that's what happened?" Mark didn't want to believe it himself but he was now becoming aware how duplicitous Julia was. "What are you going to do?" That was a question to which Mark did not know the answer.

After much agonising on what to do Mark started by making an appointment with Doctor Young. He would tell him what had happened and ask his advice. He was out of his depth and needed guidance. He hadn't given any hint to

Julia that he had seen through her ruse. He wanted to know the best way to tackle it first.

Chapter 53

"Good morning, Mark. What can I do for you?" Doctor Young welcomed Mark into his consulting room.

Mark took a deep breath and launched into his tale of Julia's exploits. Doctor Young shook his head and said that he had to be very careful what he said because of Julia's confidentiality but he understood Mark's concern. Her behaviour though was typical of a sociopath. "Sociopath?" Mark was confused, "What happened to bipolar?"

Doctor Young said, "Ah. She didn't tell you."

Mark asked for general information on what a sociopath was and what one might do with them. Doctor Young spoke about drugs and psychotherapy but admitted it was difficult to treat. He said that being aware of the condition would at least help Mark cope. What Mark was asking himself now was did he want to live the rest of his life with this amount of stress.

He reminded himself of till death us do part.

Exhausted by the thought of another round of mainly fruitless discussions Mark did not want to go home. He needed time to absorb this latest news and formulate a plan for how he would approach Julia. Reflecting on his talk with Doctor Young he was amazed at how well Julia fitted the description of a sociopath and wondered how it had not been spotted before.

Looking back Mark, once more, could trace Julia's change only as far back as their move to the cottage. He was back on that treadmill again. What was it about the place that had had such a profound effect on his wife? More research was needed, he decided. He needed something practical to do. His project was to find something about the cottage that could cause a change of personality. He would test the water again, just in case. Maybe there was something in the soil in the garden. He would check that. Was there any mould in the house?

That could affect people, he thought. His mind briefly debated the more bizarre theories like a ghostly presence but quickly dismissed them. Good, he had a list of things to do.

This was going to take some time. Mark had already taken an hour off to see Doctor Young so decided he would have to work late. Carrying out the research in his office would give him some peace and quiet. He telephoned Julia to let her know, expecting some sort of inquisition about Lucy. He was met with indifference.

The types of contamination one could find in soil were frightening. Arsenic, lead, pesticides, fertilizers and petrol. Those were the ones he would look into. Some categories simply didn't apply because of location such as industrial chemicals and being in a high traffic area. He knew as well that there was not a landfill site nearby, from the searches carried out before they bought the property.

Arsenic contamination could cause diarrhoea, headaches, drowsiness and cancers. It could also lead to poor circulation and strokes. Lead could cause hearing and vision problems, increased blood pressure and poor muscle coordination. Petrol spills could result in headaches, nausea and dizziness and fertilizers could result in cancer. Excellent, Mark had now succeeded in scaring himself half to death.

Time to employ the logical part of his brain before panic set in. He read the list of symptoms and concluded that none of them applied to Julia. He would look at mould. The search on that revealed that effects included allergies, asthma and respiratory infections. This was not what he was looking for either.

Now thoroughly depressed Mark rested his head on his desk. At this point Lucy walked in.

"Oh dear. You look down in the dumps. Let's go to the Fox and Hounds and you can tell me all about it." He stood up, put on his jacket and they left together.

Chapter 54

Mark bought a shandy and a Malibu and coke and they settled at a quiet table. Lucy had finally got Mark on his own away from the office. She sipped her drink demurely, she suspected he liked demure, and gave him her sweetest smile. "I'm having some problems with Julia," was how Mark started and Lucy frowned with concern on the outside and smiled with joy on the inside.

The conversation that followed was not at all what Lucy wanted to hear. Mark didn't want to go into specifics that would be betraying Julia's confidence, but suffice to say the issues were with her health. He was very concerned for his wife. He didn't know the best way to help her but was desperate to find some answers. Lucy nodded and grimaced in the appropriate places and she tried a bit of subtle manipulation. "Maybe there is nothing you can do." And, "Maybe she doesn't want to be helped." Mark was having none of it. Failure wasn't an option for him.

An hour later Lucy was no longer paying attention to Mark, even checking her watch at one point. Fantasy had proved to be so much better than reality. When Mark started on the effects of soil contamination on health she could stand no more. "Look at the time. I'm sorry Mark I've got to go. I hope this talk helped." He hadn't even bought her a second drink. Lucy left the pub well and truly over her infatuation. What on earth had attracted her to

Mark in the first place? He was tall and looked good in a suit. He was very conscientious at work and popular with his clients. It now seemed his popularity was more to do with his fastidious approach to work than his personality. He was boring and mean. What man worries about his wife's health and still moans about whether his shirts are ironed?

At home Mark was met by Julia who now, it seemed, had decided she was concerned about where he had been. And so the questions began. "Why did you have to work late?"

Mark was exasperated. "When I called earlier you didn't give a damn that I was working late."

"I've had time to think about it now," Julia said menacingly.

Mark resolved to take the bull by the horns. "I had some research to do. Then I went for a drink with Lucy." Mark held up his hand. "Before you go off on one she was good enough to listen to my worries about you. To reiterate I am not nor ever have been interested in Lucy in a romantic way. This visit to the pub confirmed that she is a very young empty-headed girl. Kind hearted though."

That had taken the wind out of Julia's sails. "Thank you for your candour. You always see the best in people. She wasn't being kind hearted, she was making her move. Don't ever go near that slut again."

Mark knew there was an element of truth in what Julia had said. That part of the conversation was over. Now for the really tough stuff. "I was behind at work because I took time off this morning to see Doctor Young."

Julia looked at Mark and knew that he had found out about the change in her diagnosis. She headed to the kitchen with Mark trailing behind. She poured a glass of water from the jug and sat at the table ready for the tirade. "So. You're a sociopath then." Mark had indeed discovered the truth.

"I thought my records were confidential," Julia countered.

"He thought I knew, Julia. Anyway it doesn't change the fact that you hid a very important piece of information from me."

It was a relief of sorts for Julia to be able to give up all the pretence. She wasn't going to the therapist any more, that had stopped some time ago. She wasn't going to go to Pilates any more, the girls had been pushed too far. Mark asked, implored, her to let him know important changes or facts rather than hide them. He was her husband, in sickness and in health, till death do us part. He might not like what she did but they were in it together. Julia considered his entreaty and agreed to make more of an effort. She was hoping to reignite their sex life.

Mark had not been interested recently.

A decision was taken to let people carry on thinking that Julia's problems were caused by bipolar disorder. It was more likely to make people sympathetic and understanding than the alternative. Mark certainly didn't want Maurice and Martin finding out. Their tolerance had been sorely tried already.

Chapter 55

Life was more straightforward for Julia now that she had confessed to her lies. She no longer had to remember to talk about therapy and Pilates. She was back working in the garden now, despite Mark's latest paranoia being about soil contamination. He had gone through the results of his research with her and reluctantly agreed that it was unlikely to be having an effect on her. He had examined the house from top to bottom for mould despite it being extremely unlikely to result in a neurological disorder.

As far as Julia was concerned if this was a neurological disorder she was glad she had one. A year ago she had barely been able to make a decision and had been terrified of all social situations. Now she couldn't think of anything that truly scared her. Apart from being without her water, of course. Mark must have exhausted all possible environmental hazards now. If he dredged up anything else to go on about she would lose her rag.

Once again Mark had to telephone Kelly with bad news. "So you were right. She was trying to manipulate you." Kelly warned Mark to be on his guard from now on. She also thanked him for his efforts to help her sister. Mark was some kind of saint in her eyes. She didn't know how well she would cope with Julia under the circumstances.

Maurice called Mark into his office the next morning. Oh God, thought Mark, am I going to get a lecture about fraternising with Lucy? It was a work-related matter. There was a half day conference which Maurice usually attended and this year he wanted to send Mark. It would mean travelling up in the morning, staying overnight, (the meeting didn't usually end until around 7pm,) and returning the next day. He knew that it would mean leaving Julia alone and hoped that this was not a problem.

"I could take her with me," Mark said.

Maurice pursed his lips furiously. "Do you think that's wise?" Mark explained that he would deposit Julia in the hotel room, possibly book her a spa treatment (check cost), and then take her for dinner somewhere well away from the other delegates. "Well you know your wife Mark. If you think it is....feasible then ok. I would urge you to give it some serious thought. I personally have some reservations."

Mark tried his best to reassure Maurice that it would be fine. There had been a specific complication that had led to the dinner party debacle and Julia was on medication now.

Mark did think it over, weighing up the pros and cons, and would take the precaution of having a serious talk with Julia before they went. He was not above appealing to her baser instincts so would offer a shopping trip by way of bribery on top of the spa treatments. The alternative meant leaving her alone overnight. Who knew what havoc she could wreak in that amount of time?

The logistics of the trip were the first thing on Julia's mind. When would they go? How long would they stay? There and back in 24 hours didn't sound too bad. Julia could bottle enough water to see her through that period of time. When Mark offered the spa treatments and shopping she was in. She did have to suffer a lecture on her behaviour and the potential damage to his reputation and career from Mark but she was getting used to that now.

The hotel was booked and he had, after consulting Julia, also booked a facial and massage for her. He had of course balked at the price but he had promised. Julia was in a good mood as they set off for the conference, although she did tell Mark to shut up in the car when he had been going through the day's itinerary. "I hate bloody itineraries," she had said.

They arrived at the large hotel and were directed to a room which was nice but homogenous.

Mark fussed about his notes and itinerary. He tested several pens to find one that worked and then decided to take them all. Did Julia know where the spa was? Was Julia alright? He was driving Julia round the bend. "I am absolutely fine. Go." Mark backed out of the room offering advice and cautions as he went.

Julia let out a sigh of relief. She removed her two bottles of water from her overnight bag and took a few swigs from one of them. Fortified Julia left the room in search of the spa. She was ushered into a changing room where a luxurious robe awaited her. When she emerged one of the white-coated beauticians took her to a small room with low lighting and ambient music.

What was it with the ambient music? she thought. A hairband was applied to hold back her hair which provoked the inevitable comments. "You have such beautiful hair. So thick and shiny." She had heard it all before.

Some two hours later thoroughly relaxed Julia returned to the room. She had time to hit a couple of shops before Mark was finished. A bit of makeup on her scrubbed face and then off for some retail therapy. Before she left she would have some more water.

Chapter 56

Where was the water? Julia had left it on the floor by the bed. She searched all around the bed. She searched the wardrobe, the drawers, the bathroom and then searched them all again. The bottles were gone. She sprinted to the reception desk. "I am in room 212. Someone has removed my water."

The receptionist looked perplexed. "Removed your water?"

This was not going to be easy.

Julia explained that she had brought two bottles of water with her and left them in the room while she visited the spa. On her return from the spa they were gone. Well that was easily resolved she would be given two bottles of water by the hotel without charge to replace them.

She didn't want the hotel's brand of water she wanted her water. The receptionist, Lisa, fixed her customer service smile firmly in place and promised to investigate.

Half an hour later Julia was still waiting at reception. She had sat down in the ubiquitous tub chairs, she had stood at the counter and she was now pacing up and down. Lisa reappeared with a nervous smile. Things were not looking good. Lisa explained that a member of staff had gone to the room to check the towels and toiletries and had seen the bottles on the floor.

Thinking they had been discarded she had removed them. "Have you got them then?" Julia asked. Unfortunately, the bottles had been emptied and then put out for recycling.

Somehow Julia made it back to the room without screaming. She found a paper bag to breathe into. It was now nearly four o'clock Mark would not be back for another three hours.

When he got back they would have to forego the night in the hotel and return home straight away. She repacked the clothes that they had only unpacked a few hours ago and sat and waited.

Each minute that passed felt like an hour. The uncomfortable feelings of withdrawal were beginning to appear. It was the same anxiety and physical symptoms she had endured in France. She paced the room and packed and repacked the clothes. She was desperate to find something to distract her from her increasing panic. Five o'clock, six o'clock, seven o'clock passed. When would he get back?

By the time Mark returned at 7.30 she was distraught. He had barely opened the door before she was on her feet telling him that they must go home. "Hang on. Calm down and breathe. Now, why must we go home?"

Julia looked at him with desperation. "They've taken my water."

"I don't know what that means," Mark was becoming alarmed.

It took several attempts to get an explanation from Julia that made any sense. Mark was getting more confused as Julia made ever more frantic attempts to tell him what had happened. He pieced together the story bit by bit. Julia had brought water from the pump with her and one of the hotel staff had thrown it away. She wanted, no needed, to go home because she couldn't go without her water.

Mark was about to launch into a lecture about how ridiculous this all was when he looked closely at Julia. He noticed her pallid skin and the slight sheen of sweat on her face. This is what she had looked like in Paris. Julia had sunk to her knees in front of him and was now begging him to take her home. He had already paid for the room but she was clearly in distress. They would have to go.

By the time they got in the car Julia was sobbing. It was a two hour drive. Mark imagined it would be the longest two hours of his life. Once they got going Julia became slightly calmer.

The sobbing became a pathetic whimpering accompanied by her rocking to and fro. Mark wanted to get her home as fast as possible so he broke the speed limit. Something he would never normally do.

It was nearly 10pm when they got back to the cottage. The car had hardly stopped when Julia leapt out and ran through the garden. Mark was a couple of paces behind and caught her as she reached the pump. "Julia. Stop. Think about this rationally. Tell yourself that you don't need this water. Use your willpower." Julia turned to Mark and punched him in the face.

Chapter 57

Mark was in the kitchen still trying to stop his nose bleed when Julia came in. He had left her drinking water that she had pumped into her metal cup. She was noticeably more composed.

"I can't believe you hit me," Mark said.

Julia replied, "You were getting in my way."

Mark went to bed. He was in a state of shock. Of all the possible scenarios arising from Julia's condition he had not envisaged physical violence. He did not want to become a battered husband. He would have to see Doctor Young again.

The next couple of days were full of menace. Julia glared at Mark every time he went near her and he was genuinely worried that she would hit him again. She was enjoying terrorising Mark and if he did anything truly annoying she would hit him again. At least Mark's conference had gone well. They had left the hotel amid puzzled looks from the staff but no one else had been privy to Julia's meltdown.

An appointment had been made at the doctor's and Mark was not looking forward to admitting that Julia had turned violent. His worry now was that having done it once she would do it again. He was walking on eggshells trying not to provoke her. This was not the way he was going to live his life. He hoped Doctor Young could help him find an answer to this increasingly difficult problem.

"So she thinks she's addicted to this water?" Doctor Young was trying to understand the story.

"Thinks she is or actually is. I don't know which," Mark replied. He had gone right back to the beginning and the first signs of change a year ago. The bizarre behaviour from a previously shy retiring woman, the withdrawal symptoms in Paris and the episode that had culminated in Julia hitting him. "I even had the water tested in case it was poisoning her."

It seemed that there were programs for addiction to alcohol, drugs, gambling and even sex.

Of course Julia had to be addicted to something obscure. The doctor had suggested therapy of a different kind. Cognitive Behavioural Therapy or CBT was recognised as a treatment for addictions and addictive behaviours. Mark held out little hope of getting Julia to agree to that.

He had to convince her that it was a problem first.

Over dinner Mark told Julia about his visit with Doctor Young. She rolled her eyes and carried on eating. She maintained, as he predicted, that she didn't have a problem and flatly refused to consider any further therapy whatever fancy name you gave it. "How can you say it's not a problem? Have you forgotten the state you were in the other day? Have you forgotten you hit me?" Mark appealed to Julia but she was unmoved.

"If I'm not away from the water it's not a problem."

Whether Julia was addicted to something in the water or imagined she was addicted to the water was a moot point. Her reaction to withdrawal had been very real. The cycle had to be broken somehow. Mark was now coming to the conclusion that he would have to effect a cure himself. He couldn't cut Julia off from the water and make her go cold turkey. He would wean her off gradually.

An uneasy truce was observed in the cottage over the next couple of weeks. Julia had her water and her garden and Mark had his new project. He was meticulously planning Julia's cure. He was going to take two weeks off work and devote the time to helping his wife. He had been watching Julia closely at weekends gauging how much of the pump water she was drinking. He had measured the contents of the glass she was using and calculated, as near as he could, how many centilitres of water she consumed per day. He had then calculated how much he needed to reduce the amount each day over a fourteen day period until she was having none at all. Once the process was complete he would dismantle the pump to stop any further access to the water.

The plan was good in theory but there was a lot to put in place before Mark started. He had been buying canned food and supplies and keeping them in the boot of his car. He wasn't going to be able to leave Julia alone during the process so he had to ensure he didn't have to leave the house. He had bought toiletries, including feminine ones, every type of over the counter drug, UHT milk and lots of coffee.

His plan was to send Julia to the supermarket as usual on the Saturday morning and while she was out fit a couple of steel hasps to the bedroom door so that he could padlock it and prevent her leaving. He would also cut out a section at the bottom of the door big enough to pass plates through. There was an en suite bathroom so she didn't need to leave the room at all. He couldn't believe that he was doing this. Desperate times call for desperate measures so they say.

"Are you going away while you are on leave?" Martin asked.

"No. I want to spend some time with Julia now that she is getting better." This whole thing had turned him into a liar too.

"So if we need to we can contact you?" Martin enquired.

Mark said that under normal circumstances it wouldn't be a problem but with Julia's fragile state he would rather they didn't unless it was urgent. Martin agreed.

Julia was absorbed in her own life. As long as Mark didn't get in her way or stop her drinking her water he could do what he liked. Since she had hit him he had been extremely wary and keen not to antagonise her. She wished she had hit him sooner if this was the result. Things had been quieter but now that she had the upper hand she took every opportunity to goad him. If he looked upset she would frown and say, "Poor Mark," in a mockingly sympathetic way.

She wondered if she could annoy him enough to make him retaliate by hitting her. Julia was completely unaware of what Mark was doing with his time.

Everything was set for the next two weeks. The only person Mark had advised about his plan was Kelly. He needed someone to know in case of an emergency. He had arranged to call her every evening with an update and to confirm that all was well. A missed call would mean that there was trouble. Kelly was dubious about the cause and therefore the cure for Julia's troubles. Things had got so out of control that locking her up may work because it would allow Mark to wrest the power from Julia. Being shut away and denied what she wanted may be enough to snap her out of her destructive mood. Kelly was giving Mark her full support in this enterprise in the hope that there would be a change.

Chapter 58

Julia went to the supermarket on Saturday morning. She planned to make the lamb tagine again. It had been delicious last time and she had to make an effort every now and then to keep Mark happy. Considering the revelations of the last few weeks he had been surprisingly laid back. She had been left alone to enjoy her garden and her own company. She had never wondered why Mark hadn't made more of a fuss about her lies concerning her condition. She just counted her lucky stars.

She regarded Mark with contempt now. Julia had been able to manipulate and deceive him so many times. When he wanted to try and regain some control he had called in her sister Kelly.

He knew how ambivalent she was towards her family yet he still involved her sister. He must have been desperate. That was when he wasn't running to the doctor behind her back. He couldn't handle her now so he must have decided to leave her alone. She had her water and her hobbies and if he didn't annoy her too much she would leave him alone too.

When Julia got home Mark was in the kitchen drinking coffee. He helped her put the shopping away and she talked about her plans for the evening meal. "I've been doing some DIY upstairs, come and have a look."

Julia went up the stairs and saw various dust sheets draped around. "I'd better check what you've been doing. If I don't like it you will have to change it." Julia was already determined not to like whatever he had done.

He pointed to the bedroom and said, "After you." Julia walked inside and saw some small patches of colour painted on the wall. Mark was stood in the doorway. "Have a look. Tell me which one you like best." Julia went nearer to the far wall to have a look. The door closed behind her and there were some rattling noises. She glanced back and wondered what was going on.

Something wasn't right. Julia went back to the door and found that she couldn't open it. She tried again and again and again. She was locked in. Mark had locked her in. Mark called to her through the door. "Julia. Don't panic." Of course that made her panic. Rattling on the door was having no effect.

Julia stopped trying that and started yelling. "What the fuck is going on? Why have you locked me in?" Mark told her that she needed to calm down and then he would explain. "I can't wait to hear your explanation for locking your wife in the fucking bedroom!" Julia screamed.

Although she was incensed Julia managed to gather her wits enough to want to hear Mark's reason for his actions. "Tell me," was all she said. Mark spoke at length about his concern for her welfare. He had seen her reaction when she was denied the pump water and realised that it had become an addiction. She had said that she was not going to leave the cottage again and risk being without it. When she had been without it she had lost all reason and had hit him. This addiction was having a profound effect on their lives so the time had come to get it under control. He had locked her in the room so that he could help her beat her addiction.

He would not make her go cold turkey, he would gradually reduce the amount of water she was given until she no longer needed it.

Inside the room Julia listened with a mixture of rage and terror. He wouldn't give her enough.

That was her biggest fear and her first question was, "Where is my water? I have at least eight glasses a day and I've only had two. I need some more now. NOW." She noticed the neat section cut out of the bottom of the door. Good God, Mark was going to pass her food through like she was in prison. Typical of him to think of everything. It was slowly dawning on Julia how thoroughly this must have all been planned. The locks on the door, the piece cut out of the bottom and the painting on the wall to draw her in. She had always laughed at Mark's pedantic nature, when it wasn't annoying her. She cursed him now. "Where's my WATER?"

"I will bring your first allowance of water with your lunch," Mark informed Julia.

Allowance. Julia wanted to scream. Julia did scream. She was now completely lost in her fury. To her Mark's actions were completely mad. He was the one that was crazy. He had locked her in a room to stop her drinking water. She was not going to just sit there and let him dictate what she could and could not have.

Mark removed the notorious notepad from his briefcase. He intended to keep a journal over the next two weeks. It would be valuable to note changes in her mood and help assess when she showed signs of improvement. Ultimately he hoped to note in the book the moment when he knew she was cured.

Chapter 59

Day one of the detox was underway. Mark had gone downstairs to make Julia some lunch and get her carefully measured ration of water. He marked the box on his chart so that he could keep track of how much water she had been given. Julia was apoplectic screaming and hammering on the door. It was distressing for her, he had not expected her to go quietly, but it was also distressing for him.

Mark delivered a plate of sandwiches and a small bottle half filled with her water. Julia snatched up the bottle as he rolled it into the room. She was quiet for a few seconds whilst she drank and then the ranting started again. "I hate you. I fucking hate you. How could you do this to me?" There was a brief pause. Drinking more water he imagined and then off she went again. It was going to be a long day.

Inside the bedroom Julia was veering between shock, anger and fear. The shock that Mark had locked her in the room. When did he grow a set of balls? She was furious that she had been tricked and her water consumption was now dictated by him. She was very afraid. The few hours of withdrawal which she had experienced had been torturous. She didn't want to go through that again. The only way to vent her frustration was to keep up the clamour.

The first day of captivity for Julia felt like the longest day of her life. At three o'clock she was given some water with a promise of more at six o'clock with her dinner. When she got the little bottles she drank from them immediately. She was terrified that she would knock over a bottle and waste its precious content; when her dinner arrived she immediately started drinking and eventually looked at her evening meal. The food looked fine it was the plastic knife and fork which provoked her anger this time.

"A plastic knife and fork. What do you think I'm going to do you stupid bastard, tunnel my way out? How long am I going to be locked in here?" They gave you plastic knives and forks if you were suicidal or a nutcase didn't they? Julia wondered which one Mark thought she was. He had taken two weeks off work and so that meant that her sentence was likely to be the same.

What would he do at the end of two weeks? If he let her out then what was to stop her going back to drinking the water?

A whole new set of worries had occurred surrounding the water source. Would Mark do something to the pump? Julia started yelling again. She was panicking thinking about what Mark would do while she was locked in the room. "What are you doing out there? I want to know what you are doing. Mark. Mark. MARK."

Another thing to fret about. Julia tried to breathe deeply and calm down but the thought of him destroying the pump was making her break out in a cold sweat. The bedroom window didn't overlook the pump so she wouldn't be able to see what he was doing. The not knowing what was happening outside the room made her imagination run riot. She also realised that she did not have a friend anywhere who would wonder where she was. She had thought that she didn't need anybody and that having friends was too much hard work. She screamed in rage again at her own short-sightedness.

Mark did indeed have plans for the pump but he could do nothing until he no longer needed the water. The last few days of his two week break would be spent digging down round the pipe and then cutting it off and capping it. He would then fill the hole and there would then be no way to access the water. He had decided against just removing the hand pump on top of the pipe. Mark always wanted to do a thorough job.

That first night would be etched on Mark's memory forever. Julia was either calling his name and shouting or hammering on the door and the walls. Neither of them got much sleep. The next day dawned with nerves frayed on both sides of the bedroom door. It was three o'clock in the morning before Julia exhausted herself and finally went quiet. At seven o'clock she began shouting again. "Where's my fucking water?"

Journal: Day one. As expected Julia has objected to being locked in the bedroom. She has displayed her anger by shouting repeatedly and banging on the door. Most of her comments concern the water. She is worried that she will not be given enough and she is also worried about what will happen to the pump itself. No other questions have occurred to her she is completely absorbed by thoughts of the water. I have had very little sleep due to Julia shouting and banging the walls and door. I have rung Kelly and informed her that the plan has commenced and she was not surprised by Julia's furious reaction.

Day two was a repeat of day one with the addition of Julia stabbing at Mark's hand with a plastic knife when he delivered her food. His decision to not use normal cutlery had proved correct. She couldn't do much harm with the knife but her attempts were vicious. After the first time Mark had been more careful about pushing her food through the gap and the fact that she couldn't do more damage enraged her further.

Around and around the room Julia paced. She had made an exhaustive search of the room only to discover that Mark had removed any metal or sharp objects. No nail scissors or tweezers. No hair clips or tie pins. Even her jewellery had been removed from the room. Mark had, as usual, been meticulous in his preparations, damn him.

In the bathroom she found an old electric shaver. It wouldn't get her out of the room but it would allow her to express her rage and define her identity. She had changed from dull Julia who had no personality. The only noteworthy thing about her back then had been her hair. So many compliments. It was thick and shiny. It was lustrous. The number of times she had heard the words crowning glory, well she couldn't even count. She was a person not just a head of hair. People had talked about it because there was nothing else to say about her.

Julia shaved off her hair. It was so liberating to be free of it. Her hair had been detracting from the real Julia underneath. She studied her reflection and smiled. People would notice her now and Mark would hate it. A job well done. She collected up all the hair and piled it onto the plate ready to hand back to Mark.

In between bouts of shrieking Mark tried to sleep on the sofa. The periods of quiet were welcome but as time passed he began fretting about her wellbeing. He had removed all sharp objects and he had also removed ties belts scarves and dressing gown cords. Would she be suicidal? Mark didn't think she would but he had taken every precaution just in case.

At regular intervals during the day Julia would call out demanding her water. Her new ravings were about what she was going to do when she got out. "I am gonna kill you when I get out. Good job you didn't give me a real knife because I would stab you. I would definitely stab you. And

228

take great pleasure in it." Mark hoped this detox worked or he was in a whole lot of trouble.

In those moments Julia was very serious about her death threats. Mark had overreacted to the situation as usual. It was because he couldn't control her any more. He wanted her calm and compliant and she was not prepared to let him do this to her when she had done nothing wrong. She had changed but it was for the better. She was now confident, self-sufficient and enjoying herself. Once he was out of the picture she could live exactly as she pleased. She began planning for a different future when she would be alone.

On reaching the top of the stairs with Julia's dinner Mark noticed a plate had been pushed back through the gap in the door. It had something on it. As Mark neared he could see it was a pile of hair.

"Julia what have you done?"

She was laughing, "I've got rid of all that hair which was weighing me down. I'm a person not a head of hair."

Mark took the plate away shaking his head sadly. She would regret doing that when she was better.

Mark felt a great sadness when he removed her beautiful hair from the plate. It had been so much a part of her identity. He put the long strands in a plastic bag. He had no idea what he was going to do with it but he could not bear to throw it away. He had heard her words, "I'm a person not a head of hair," and he could see what she meant. It was the first thing that people noticed about her and the first thing they commented on. Now the focus would have to be on her personality. He sat down at the kitchen table with the bag of hair in front of him and found himself close to tears.

Journal: Day two. There has been slightly less shouting and banging today, probably because she is tired. She attacked my hands with the plastic knife and along with shouting about the water she has made threats to kill me. There have been periods of calm. During one of these she has shaved her head. The hair was passed out of the room on a plate. This makes me very sad, she had such beautiful hair. The water reduction is going according to plan. She has not complained about having withdrawal symptoms. Kelly was upset about the head shaving when I told her.

Day three Mark felt a little better having got about four hours' solid sleep. Julia had slept too and now the clamour for her water started afresh. Was it his imagination or was she not quite as manic as the day before? Mark headed for the kitchen to prepare breakfast and measure some water for Julia.

During day three Mark had time to reflect on everything that had led him to this drastic action.

Whichever way he looked at it the onset of the problems was linked somehow to their move to the cottage. He had carried out all the tests he could think of on their environment, a carbon dioxide detector being the latest addition, and had found nothing. Logic dictated that he was wrong about his fears but he could not shake his suspicions. He had taken to walking out into the garden and staring at the pump as if waiting for some explanation to be revealed to him.

The pump was becoming an obsession to him as well.

Journal: Day three. Definitely less noise from her today. If I approach the room she still shouts obscenities and she still reminds me, by yelling, when her next ration of water is due. The quieter periods give me time to think about what I am doing and I find that I am more determined than ever to see this through. I have spoken to Kelly and reported her slightly calmer state.

Chapter 60

Day four saw a change in tactics from Julia. The screaming and shouting and threats were replaced by crying and begging. "I'm sorry I said those things. I understand what you are trying to do now, let me out and I'll be good." Julia was tired of yelling and getting nowhere.

She had stopped reacting out of panic and was now thinking about other ways to get out of her prison. Mark had expected her to try this at some stage and hardened his heart against her entreaties. He had to carry his plan through to its conclusion.

The anticipated withdrawal pain had not materialised but that was small comfort for Julia. She was still locked in a room against her will with her jailer calling all the shots. The changes to her over the months included ever increasing self-determination. This was now being taken away and she was going to fight for her rights in any way she could. On day four that meant begging and pleading. As demeaning as it felt it was a means to an end.

As she begged and cried Julia hated Mark even more for making her act in this way. Her murderous thoughts were to the fore and she was mentally making plans for how she would dispatch him. She would claim that he was the mad one as evidenced by him locking her in the room and would tearfully explain how she had no alternative but to kill him to escape. He had made threats to her she would say and everyone would be sympathetic to her ordeal and understand why she had to resort to violence. Of course, she would inform them, she had only meant to injure him but had been given no choice in the end.

The day was quieter than the previous ones but no less traumatising. Hearing his wife cry and beg was harrowing for Mark. Julia promised to be good. She promised to cooperate with Mark's weaning procedure. He probably needed her help in the kitchen and around the house, she would do that too. After a while she would lose her temper and start cursing him and then apologise and be contrite again.

This pattern repeated itself a number of times but there were periods of calm too. Mark tried to keep busy around the house to distract himself from the stress. He was organising the CDs, books and DVDs into alphabetical order. He had gone through kitchen drawers and cupboards and thrown away old food and the general detritus people collect. Julia wouldn't be happy about it but that was the least of his worries.

He was standing looking at the pump again. Mark could barely remember walking out to the garden. While there he collected some water and looked forward to starting work on its demise in a few days' time. He gave it a last stare and smiled. He was going to end this battle and he and Julia were going to be the winners.

Journal: Day four. A very difficult day. She is crying and begging to be released. She is offering all kinds of promises if she is let out. I had expected this stage during the detox but it is hard to listen to one's wife sobbing. She still questions me about the water whenever I am near the room. Her plates come back empty so I assume that she is eating properly. She has not asked for anything other than water. Books and magazines are in the room for her and I have supplied plenty of clothes. Kelly is sympathetic to my distress at hearing Julia beg and admits that she probably couldn't remain steadfast in the circumstances. She has offered to visit but I feel that her presence may be troubling for Julia.

There was another attempt to get out of the room the next day. Day five brought calls for Mark from Julia. She wasn't demanding water. Her voice was weaker and faltering. She was ill she said. She needed to get out and visit the doctor or the hospital. Mark informed her that, if necessary, he would call Doctor Young who was aware of the action that Mark was taking. He could treat her in the room. Unless she was dying she was not getting out.

When Mark took Julia her breakfast he asked how she was feeling. "A little better," she said quietly before adding, "you've thought of everything haven't you?" Mark hoped that he had. He hadn't told Doctor Young about the detox but his bluff had paid off. He wondered what else Julia would throw at him before this whole thing was over. The rest of the day was reasonably quiet which was every bit as unnerving as the fits of anger. Mark sat downstairs wondering what Julia was doing.

Upstairs Julia was trying to think of a new strategy. Mark was so maddeningly thorough she was not sure she could find a way out of the room before the two weeks were up. What would she find when she emerged if she couldn't get out early? She doubted the pump would still be there. She thought the only way she could gain freedom was to convince Mark that his plan had worked.

Journal: Day five. Today she tried to convince me that she was ill in an attempt to get out. I had anticipated this ruse and told her that Doctor Young would come to her (not true). She accepted my lie and has been calmer since. Still asking for water but mainly quiet. The reduction of water continues as per my schedule. I will call Kelly as usual and advise her of the latest developments including her claim of illness.

On day six Mark delivered Julia's breakfast and water and received a polite, "Thank you," from inside the room followed by, "perhaps we can have a talk at some time today?" And then, laughing, "You know where to find me when you're ready." Mark walked away from the door promising to return later. He felt hopeful that they were making progress but was still wary of Julia's artifice.

Midmorning Mark took Julia a cup of coffee and sat on the floor outside of the bedroom. "OK, I'm here if you're ready to talk." He heard her sit down on the other side of the door.

"I've been thinking about this incarceration you've so cleverly engineered. I'm not happy about it but I am beginning to see why you did it." Julia told Mark that her mind was starting to clear and this had given her the opportunity to consider what had happened on the lead-up to this and why he had locked her up. Having rushed into previous attempts to escape Julia now planned to play a longer game. By the evening of the eighth day she hoped to be out of the bedroom.

She planned a gradual return to her old self, if she could remember that person, marvelling at how crazy she had been and how pleased she now was that Mark had acted so drastically.

"You understand why I'm doing this then?" Mark wanted to hear Julia confess to her addiction but they were not even halfway through yet.

Julia's reply let him know that they were not home and dry. "Because you think that I'm addicted to the water and this will help me get over it." Julia heard his sigh and knew that she had played it exactly right. Tomorrow would bring a new realisation of her condition which she would disclose to Mark indicating her improvement. "I think I'm going to have a rest now," she said as she got up and moved away from the door.

A good day's work, Julia thought to herself. How surprised he would be when she got out and dealt with him. She would remain calm as he let her out of the room. She would thank him for his help and marvel at his resilience in the face of her ravings. She would need to get to the kitchen where she could arm herself with a knife and she would then strike when he was least expecting it. She wasn't exactly relishing the thought of murdering her husband but it had to be done.

Journal: Day six. The first sign of reason today. She asked to talk and we had a conversation about why I had locked her up in which she acknowledged I was trying to help. Only day six though. Too early for a cure to have been effected and she is not accepting that she is addicted. Hopefully the next few days will produce the results I am hoping for. I have discussed the conversation we had with Kelly and she has advised caution. I am inclined to agree with her.

Julia had been going over and over in her head what she would say on what was now day seven. Mark brought her breakfast and her ever decreasing allocation of water. "Thank you. Mark, don't go. I want to talk to you again." Julia had slept well the night before, she said. The best night's sleep she had had for a long time, not just since she had been locked up. She admitted that she had done some pretty crazy things and been hurtful to him and others. She also wondered about her extreme reaction at being away from her water and speculated whether it was a metaphor for some other trouble in her life.

Closer to acceptance but not quite there. Julia's little disclosure would give Mark hope and might even make him think that the whole water thing was a red herring. To reinforce that she added, "I don't know if gaining clarity is a result of reducing the water or simply giving myself the time for some introspection. I know that I'm not liking what I see." Mark listened carefully to what she said and replayed their conversations in his head over and over. He was well aware that a game of cat and mouse was being played.

Journal: Day seven. More conversation, today focusing on her realisation that her behaviour has been bad. Still in denial about the role of the water. She is trying to blame something other than the water. I believe this is called deflection. The physical act of locking her up was relatively easy. I suspect that the mental changes she is going through will be the challenging part. I am beginning to wonder if I am equipped to cope with what is to come. Still resolved to complete the course of detox fully. I have noted that she is using less bad language and is not asking for water but continues to snatch at it as it is passed through. I have rung Kelly as usual to say that all is well.

The comments Julia was making showed a growing self-awareness but she was still in denial about the water. Mark could see real signs of improvement but was determined to see this thing through to the end. Not until Julia had gone a couple of days without any water would he be happy.

Chapter 61

All along Mark's plan had been to have Julia completely off the water by day twelve and then on the fourteenth day he could reveal to her that she had already been free of its grip for two days. A couple of her rations had already been tap water not pump water.

Day eight had arrived and they were now more than halfway through. Mark had passed breakfast to Julia and said good morning. The sound from the room was that of someone who had been crying. A sniff or two and a croaky, "Good morning."

"Are you alright?" asked Mark.

"This clarity thing is all very well but I'm having to remember the terrible things I've done. Mark, I was shoplifting." Julia smiled on the other side of the door and congratulated herself on another fine performance.

As Julia mentioned the shoplifting she was looking at the infamous gold dress that had caused such a furore at the dinner party. It was tacky but she had enjoyed wearing it and seeing Maurice and Martins' reactions. She now knew it was wrong to shoplift (where had that thought come from?) but it had meant that she had acquired that dress. It would have been a greater crime to pay for it.

For the first time Mark felt genuinely sorry for Julia. She was having to face up to some appalling things. She must be racked with guilt. Not exactly racked with guilt but Julia did feel uncomfortable when she recalled some of her more excessive behaviour. Her conscience which had been dormant for a while was waking up.

When Mark delivered her lunch Julia launched into what she hoped would be her final gambit.

"Mark. I need to say something." The cracking voice as if on the edge of tears was employed.

"I'm here Julia." Mark waited for her to start.

There was some coughing and sniffing as she composed herself and then, "You were right. I've been addicted to that water." Mark remained silent hoping she would embellish on this announcement.

Julia declared that she could now see how insane she must have seemed. She apologised for the dinner party, the swearing, the rudeness and the shoplifting. How would she ever face those people she had hurt again? She would have to visit the others and beg their forgiveness. Mark listened but was not entirely convinced. His formerly shy wife would rather die than visit people to offer an apology. She would never have done something for which she had to apologise.

The final part of her plan was coming soon. The admittance of her addiction was what Mark wanted to hear. If all went well she would be having dinner in the kitchen and she and Mark would be talking calmly about her problems. She would confess to taking things too far and would promise to only drink four glasses of water a day. This compromise would hopefully work. If not she would have to kill Mark.

It was on delivery of dinner that Julia said the words Mark had been expecting. "Now that I'm better and facing the truth I could really do with your complete support. Let me out and you can then help me rehabilitate before you go back to work." Julia was met by silence, not the jangling of keys as he rushed to unlock her prison. "Mark? What do you think?" Don't panic, she told herself.

After what seemed like an eternity Mark spoke. "I can't let you out yet Julia. It's too soon."

Rage bubbled to the surface. Julia had wasted three days sucking up to Mark saying what he wanted to hear. All to no avail. "You bastard. I've said that I'm sorry. I've cut down on the water and played your little game. What more do you want?"

"I want my wife back," stated Mark before he walked away. She was angry now. Talking about her misdemeanours had made her think about them and she was now feeling decidedly uncomfortable. She had been so convinced that she was right and everyone else was wrong but now she wasn't so sure.

Journal: Day eight. Another attempt was made today to get out of the room. She did this by claiming she was cured. I have had to be very careful, analysing what she is saying to divine the truth. The woman in the room is still more bad Julia than good Julia. The fact that she tried to trick me is proof of that. I am however hopeful because there are signs of change. The water reduction is on track and the next couple of days should see a bigger change. I have informed Kelly of Julia's attempt to be let out of the room and she has counselled me to stay strong. I appreciate our conversations each evening. It is the one piece of sanity in this whole crazy endeavour.

The next day Julia was very quiet and Mark had difficulty getting any response from her at all. Maybe the last failure had knocked the fight out of her and real progress could now be made.

At lunchtime he initiated a conversation. "You're quiet today. Are you OK?"

He heard her move towards the door and sit down on the other side. "I really don't know where to start," Julia said, before she tried to describe how she was now feeling. She told him she knew it was going to be hard for him to believe anything she said as she had lied so much. Not just since she had been in the room but way before that too. She was disgusted with herself for the lies and so much more. She had been thinking about her family and how awful that Christmas had been. The family wasn't ideal, what family was, but they were all she had. Mark could tell Julia was crying at this point. Not the showy am dram tears of the past few days.

He listened and felt his heart clench in his chest. "You have done awful things Julia but nothing that can't be put right. I will be there with you through every step."

Inside the room Julia was genuinely mortified about her actions. Certain scenarios, Christmas, the dinner party and the way she had spoken to her friends replayed themselves over and over again. Each time she felt the shame of what she had done and said. Previously she had viewed her transgressions as being carried out by bad Julia. She was the guilty party. It had been easier to live with it that way. Now came the acceptance that she couldn't separate herself from those deeds. She had to take responsibility and it hurt.

Leaving her parents' house on Christmas Day was a particularly vivid memory. The caring hug on the doorstep from parents who had always seemed too busy for her touched a nerve. She had behaved appallingly to her sisters and ruined the day and yet they had been concerned for her not angry. In her miserable life before the water she had

241

told herself that her parents didn't care about her but that was untrue. Julia was the one who didn't care about Julia.

Would she really have killed Mark if she had got out of the room a couple of days ago? In the state she was in then the answer was yes. This provoked some very uncomfortable feelings in Julia. What kind of madness had made her even consider hurting Mark? She tried to push the thought away but something had made her act like a madwoman. Could it really all be down to the water she had been drinking?

Journal: Day nine. For the first time today she showed genuine remorse for her actions. She cried real tears and felt real shame. It was heart-breaking to hear but I think this was a turning point. I can only conclude that the effect of the water is wearing off allowing the true Julia to emerge. This is a worry because she will be very upset at the things she has done. I have spent a lot of time outside the room today reassuring her that she will get through this and everything will return to normal. Kelly and I are worried about the effect this realisation will have on Julia mentally in the days and weeks to come.

Chapter 62

The wall chart had been updated and noted next to the heading 'Day Ten' was 'begin excavating pump'. Breakfast had been delivered to Julia and discussions had, again, focused on her regret. She was having a hard time comprehending the mayhem she had caused and the reason for doing it. She could not fathom what had possessed her to hurt people so badly.

Was that her true nature?

Mark comforted Julia as best he could. She had done those things whilst her mind was disturbed. The real Julia would never have done those things and when she was better everybody would see what an unassuming pleasant person she was. He made her promise to work on forgiving herself and headed to the garden to dig.

An unassuming pleasant person. That was how Mark had described Julia. That is exactly what she had been and what she was becoming again. She would miss certain aspects of bad Julia. Her ability to make friends. Her determination to not be downtrodden. The way she could laugh at situations which had once, and would again, be difficult for her. The terrible things she had done and said were haunting her and she wouldn't miss those. The way she had thrown insults around was terrible. Telling Zoe she was bossy. Criticising Emily and Claire (formerly known as the clones) and accusing Faith of betraying her. And Donna. Poor Donna who was so sweet and had got the worst of it.

She physically shook at the thought of what she might have done to Mark had she been given the opportunity. He was trying to help her and she had been quite prepared to stop him with violence. She had punched him when they returned from the conference but that was nothing compared to what she had planned in the room in those first few days. She was shivering again not because of withdrawal but with the terror of what she planned.

Julia was forced to think about what she had actually done to Mark. She had been so rude to a man who had only ever shown her kindness. He wasn't weak and pathetic he was tolerant and resilient and ultimately strong enough to help her with this drastic action. Others may have shied away from doing what was necessary but Mark hadn't. She had been rude to him and made him eat liver. She had punched him in the face. The thought of the dinner party and the aftermath made her shudder with horror all over again.

Her life before discovering the water also gave her cause for concern. She could picture herself being introduced to Maurice and Martin for the first time. She blushed if they looked at her and blushed more if they spoke to her. It was the same with all strangers. Not wanting to go through the agony of socialising she had imposed her own exile. Filling her life with Pilates and friends had given her less time for introspection. She had still thought fleetingly about not being able to have children but with the return of good Julia would come the return of her negative thoughts.

Once bad Julia had been completely exorcised what would be left? Not much, she concluded.

The apathy which had been present before would soon return and then it would be too late to decide her own fate. She would have to think very carefully about returning to her old life.

Julia had kept pieces of the plastic cutlery that she had broken on Mark's hand when she had attacked him. She had been experimenting with the window lock and thought that she may be able to get it open. Mark was not going to let her out before the fourteen days were up. Her decision now was whether she stayed the course and retreated into herself or whether she fought back while she still could.

In the garden Mark stared down at the hated water pump and took great delight in driving the spade into the soil next to it. He was on leave from work and as usual that meant that it had been raining a lot. It hadn't mattered as he had nowhere to go. The ground was soft and muddy which made his job dirty but it was easier than digging out dry hard earth. He spent an hour digging strenuously. It felt good to be out of the house and carrying out physical work.

He glanced at the pump every now and then and smiled. Victory was close. Julia was on the mend and the pipe was gradually being revealed to him, ready for its final destruction.

After lunch Mark waited fifteen minutes for his food to settle and then returned to his dig. He had made a large hole at the front and would continue round leaving access on one side.

When he had collected the last of the water he needed he would remove the last piece and then climb into the pit and saw the pipe off. He had made good progress because of the soft earth and thought if he pushed hard the next day he would be all but finished.

The bedroom window didn't afford Julia a view of the pump but she knew Mark was in the garden and she was concerned about what he was doing. His absence gave her an opportunity to work on the lock. She had nearly had it a couple of times and she was going to persevere until it was open. If the lock was undone she could get out of the window. It was a bit of a drop to the ground but she could make it. She wasn't sure she wanted to escape but having the lock open would give her options.

Journal: Day ten. Water reduction continues. She is still beset by worries about what she has done. She is very quiet, much more like the Julia that I remember from before. When this is all over I may suggest therapy to help her come to terms with her guilt. I had anticipated many things but not this. It seems obvious now that she would suffer having been so reserved previously, her misdeeds must be truly shocking. Kelly is glad that my cure seems to be working and she is looking forward to seeing us when this is all over.

Ten years before, Mark and Julia had been newlyweds moving into a small two bedroomed semi-detached house in their home town. The wedding had been fairly low key due to Julia's terror of being the centre of attention. Their immediate families had attended together with a couple of Mark's university friends and a few work colleagues. Julia had worn a pretty understated dress which was fitted at the waist and gently flaring at the bottom. Her hair was loose with a small white flower pinned at one side.

Mark had loved the simplicity of Julia's wedding outfit. She wore the white ballerina length dress with a full veil to hide behind. She was such an attractive girl that she didn't need much adornment. He had worn a lounge suit (new) and they had held their reception at a nearby pub which had a small function room. They had decided to have outside caterers. It was not wise to leave food preparation to Julia or her mother. The day had been quiet but joyful and they had looked forward to their life together in the future.

Then it all started to go wrong. Julia's infertility had been the catalyst that had sent them down the route to depression and resignation. Once the possibility of having a family was taken away they had stopped hoping for anything. Mark had let her withdraw into herself. He thought now about what he could have done differently. Instead of letting Julia fade into apathy he should have found other things to help her occupy her time. As soon as she had given up work she gave up on life.

After this cure there would have to be changes to their lifestyle. Julia would have to go back to Pilates. Her friends would soon see the remarkable change in her and accept her back into the fold. They would get a dog so that Julia would have to get up in the morning and attend to its needs. She couldn't mope around for half the day if she had something to care for. When she was free of the water he would tell her about his plans so that she had something to look forward to.

Day eleven. This was the day that Mark would finish his excavation and this was the day that Julia would choose her fate. She could either disappear quietly or break out of her prison and reclaim her life. Mark was digging furiously when he hit something at the bottom of his now deep pit. He had dug down about four feet. His spade tested the soil around the obstacle and he found other resistance too. He bent down and brushed away the soil up close to the pipe.

He uncovered a bone.

To his horror, as Mark explored further, he exposed a skeleton lying at the bottom of the pit. It appeared to be curled around the pipe. He was no expert but it seemed to be very old. There was no sign of clothing and the bones were bare. What would he do now? He would have to inform the police but how would he explain his wife being locked in the bedroom? He went inside and made a cup of tea.

Chapter 63

Elizabeth stood looking at John. She was holding her face where he had slapped her. Henry had raised his voice to her a couple of times. Her father had once shaken her when she had pushed her brother in the pond. She had never been chastised more than that and did not know about men hitting women. She was stunned. John left the house with an accusatory, "You made me do it."

Thoughts of her fine house and her beautiful clothes ran through Elizabeth's mind and she considered running home straight away. A stubborn streak ran through her though and she couldn't quite bring herself to be the first to capitulate. Henry had ridden past the cottage a number of times over the last few days and she was sure that she was winning. He had not expected her to live like this for so long and was probably wondering if she would go home at all left to her own devices.

There was also the issue of the water pump. John was defying her. He was a farm worker and she was the lady of the manor. She wasn't going to leave the cottage until he completed his task as he had promised to do so many times. She thought that when he returned he would be ashamed of hitting her and he would redouble his efforts to complete the work.

John headed for the tavern. He had felt bad about hitting Elizabeth, who was a proper lady, but she had deserved it. He was working a full day on the farm and then working on the cottage in the evening. He had dug down and drilled and was now sinking a pipe into the ground. He would be finished as soon as he could get the money to pay for the hand pump to go on top. When the pump was complete there would be a new project that she would be going on about thought John. He was really beginning to regret this whole thing.

He looked round the room at the tavern but John couldn't see Molly anywhere. He fully regretted hitting her. She was a good girl. No airs and graces and demands like Elizabeth.

Sometimes when Elizabeth talked to him he barely understood what she was saying, her language was so fancy. He couldn't imagine her drinking beer or paddling in the stream like Molly did. Why had he let himself be led astray? He kept thinking of Molly laughing and Molly with a mug of cider in her hand. He thought of their kisses and of her pushing his hands away when he tried to reach inside her clothes. Finally, he thought of her walking away after he had hit her.

When they had first been exiled to the cottage John had wondered how he would cope financially. He now had to feed two people and pay for the building repairs. Back at the stable yard he was often invited to dine with the families of other workers in return for supplying them with some animal feed or a piglet or whatever else he could pilfer. That had left him with spare money for beer and gambling. He hadn't dared take anything now that he was under such close scrutiny by Henry Hunter.

Damn that Elizabeth and her big blue eyes, she had cost him dear. John had lost his spacious accommodation, his perks, his money which he was spending on repairs and his

Molly. He would have to say sorry when he returned home, she was his boss's wife, but she better not push him anymore. John was now considering packing up his belongings and moving away.

He wanted time to make a plan before he rushed into any decisions. The village was all he had ever known. It would be a while until John received his next wages so he wasn't going to leave until then anyway.

He had drunk a few beers but couldn't afford any more so he would have to go home. The question of money had arisen with Elizabeth but she had no access to any, she claimed.

Previously if she had wanted anything she simply asked, or begged depending on how expensive it was, Henry and it appeared. Her answer of course had been for him to not buy so much beer.

On arriving home John would try again to squeeze some money out of Elizabeth. He didn't believe that she had none. "If you ask Mr Hunter for help he'll give you some money." John had laid his cards on the table and admitted he couldn't afford to keep them and repair the cottage on his pay.

"Oh what a very good idea. I'll just call at the manor, remind him that I'm his wife, and ask for some money so that my lover and I can live in comfort. It's so preposterous."

Preposterous, I'll give her preposterous, thought John. He felt better after he had kicked her.

Chapter 64

Every day Elizabeth went outside to investigate the site of the pump. "Is it nearly finished?" she asked. John said it just needed the hand pump. "Well get one then," she demanded. They didn't have enough money. In fact, they didn't have any money.

Elizabeth retreated to the bedroom. They still slept together and made love. They shared a passion for the physical and this alone had made their strange alliance last for so long. She closed the door and retrieved her jewellery from its hiding place. There were pieces there which were family heirlooms and some items to which she was not so attached. She selected a brooch to give to John. He could sell it to raise the money they needed.

She thought he would be pleased with her offering but Elizabeth was now very afraid. "You've had this all this time and now you hand it over and expect me to be grateful." John's fists were clenched and he was moving menacingly toward her.

"I can get some more jewellery," Elizabeth pleaded. She felt she was bargaining for her life. John stopped his advance and considered her words. Since their first few days in the cottage, when Elizabeth was playing house, she had rarely bothered to tidy up. Her belongings were scattered throughout the house, particularly the bedroom, and whilst he was familiar with most of it he had never seen any jewellery. Where had she conjured that up from? Was there more of it?

One step at a time John said to himself. He would travel to town the next day and sell the brooch and see how much it made. Elizabeth was probably holding the good stuff back. "You make me so angry sometimes. I forget that you don't see things the same way because of how you were brought up. This brooch will make life a lot easier." That was what John considered an apology. He never liked hitting her but she made him lose control. This time he was glad he hadn't lashed out. He was chasing a pot of gold.

John was the third child of five born to his farm labourer father and mother. He had been a strong child and had fought his way to adulthood. Two of his siblings had succumbed to infant diseases and had died. Life for him was a battle and he was determined to win. He fought with his father who had fought with his mother and now he fought with anyone who stood in his way. He had an affinity with animals, particularly horses, and had made a living from skill and hard work. He doubted that Elizabeth had ever done anything that could be called work until she was banished to the cottage.

The concept of money and what things cost was alien to Elizabeth. The comments she made to John showed her ignorance. He couldn't imagine what it must have been like to grow up in a warm loving family home. She should be soft and compliant but something had gone wrong with her. Elizabeth was greedy and demanding and unforgiving. She was also beautiful and wanton. He veered between wanting her and hating her.

She had got away without a beating. Elizabeth was very relieved. It was alarming how quickly she had accepted his aggression as normal. He wasn't exactly solicitous after he hit her but he would show her some act of kindness.

Rubbing her sore feet or bringing home some wild flowers. The argument would be forgotten and forgiven. When the pump was fitted she would think about returning to Henry if he hadn't already relented and made the first move. This latest incident had frightened her more than previous incidents.

The brooch fetched good money even from the dubious character he found to sell it to. This boded well for any other pieces he could prise out of Elizabeth. He reluctantly spent a lot of the money on the pump but he had to keep in her good graces until he had found the rest of her jewellery. He knew it had to be close at hand. Of course there was money left over for a visit to the tavern and enough to buy a few bottles to take home.

In the garden John was finally fitting the hand pump. He finished off another beer, it was thirsty work. Elizabeth stood and watched with a critical eye. "All this time walking miles to get water and that's all you had to do. Stick that pump thing on top. I'd have given you the brooch ages ago if I'd known. The amount of damage walking up and down that lane has done to my shoes..." John hit her round the head as hard as he could with the spade.

Elizabeth slumped into the hole John had dug. Blood was flowing from a wound as he studied her impassively. He hit her a couple more times to ensure that she was dead and then began covering the body. The beer had numbed him slightly and had made it easier to deliver the coup de grace. How convenient that she had fallen into the hole. A ready-made grave.

John entered the cottage and opened a beer and sat at the kitchen table. That had not been planned and now he would have to clear out sooner than he had intended. He found a couple of sacks and started picking up Elizabeth's clothes and shoes and other items he could sell.

He threw his own meagre possessions in and then set about finding the jewellery.

He had thought hard about where Elizabeth may have hidden her hoard. John had remembered her trunk being delivered and then struggling to carry it upstairs. It must be hidden in the bedroom. He checked under the mattress and in her trunk but found nothing.

He then went to the chest of drawers. He pulled out the drawers and emptied the contents onto the bed ready to search through them. He could now see the floor under the chest and something caught his eye. There was a pouch resting there.

The pouch contained rings, brooches, pearls and a locket. John could not even estimate how much they were worth. The rings had precious stones. Diamonds and rubies. He was suddenly a wealthy man. He was also a murderer. Time was of the essence so he put everything back into the pouch and threw that into one of the sacks. He took one last look around the cottage to make sure he hadn't missed anything of value and then walked away.

Chapter 65

On the road John begged items of food and slept in barns and stables. He didn't want to sell any of the jewellery until he got to a city. He doubted that anyone would find Elizabeth's body, they would have assumed they had both left, but he didn't want to leave any clues just in case. His first objective was to get as far from the village as he could.

He got employment in the nearest city at a tavern. He was a strong man and he worked moving barrels and sweeping the floor and breaking up the brawls. He was poorly paid but it was a temporary job until he could cash in the jewellery. His plan was to stay in the city for a while until he got the lie of the land. Working at the tavern meant he rubbed shoulders with criminals and as he befriended some of them he discovered the best places to sell his goods.

He sold some of the rings for a good price and then packed up and moved on. John worried that word of his windfall would reach the criminals he knew and then he would be a target.

When he reached the next city he did the same again. Lowly paid job, research the criminal underground and then sell some gold. He had a plan and stuck to it. He wasn't the brightest man but he was a determined man and nothing was going to make him deviate from his course.

Before he left the latest city John invested in some decent clothes and some well-made boots.

He arrived in the next city, his final destination, as a wealthy gentleman. He had left the fields and farmland of the south behind and was now on the border of Scotland. Far enough away not to run into anyone from his former life. John used his money wisely and playing to his strengths he bought livestock and a smallholding and bred fine horses for fine gentlemen like himself. He had acquired a wife who was meek and obedient. He had never had to hit her. He had two sons, Mark and Matthew, who were strong and healthy and inherited their father's love of horses.

Only occasionally did John think back to the day when he had killed Elizabeth. It was so long ago now it was as if it hadn't really happened. He felt no remorse and had convinced himself that Elizabeth had been a benefactor who had allowed him to live a better more productive life through her death. He sometimes wondered what happened to her little dog Pip.

Chapter 66

Mark was in a quandary. There was a skeleton in his garden and a wife locked up in the house. And now it started raining. The downpour washed away the dirt from the skeleton revealing more of the bones.

He had returned to the kitchen to consider carefully what his next move should be. He was so close to the end of the detox he couldn't give up now. He also couldn't cover up the skeleton which had been his first thought. Mark was a slave to his morals and ethics so he knew he would contact the police. Not today though. He would sleep on it tonight and then tomorrow would see Julia given her last few drops of her special water. He could have changed his schedule of water reduction but it had worked so far and they were so close to the end.

That evening when he phoned Kelly to check in he advised her about his horrific find.

"Have you phoned the police?" Kelly's first question jangled Mark's nerves even more.

"Not yet." Kelly was worried. He explained that he was close to finishing Julia's detox and he couldn't stop now. It would be a nightmare convincing the police that he had locked her up for her own good. At least if she was fully cured she could corroborate his story. He promised that he was planning to call in the morning.

Revealing the presence of the skeleton to Julia would not be a good idea, Mark decided. She was very fragile at the moment and he didn't want to disturb her further. Julia was in the bedroom with her improvised lock picks working patiently at the problem. If she could just open the lock the choice of how she lived would be hers.

Journal: Day eleven. Julia is more and more like her old self. She is quiet and compliant and is no longer referring to the water at all. I have been distracted by a gruesome discovery by the pump. A skeleton has been unearthed. I have resolved to tell the police tomorrow when Julia's detox is complete. Their presence will keep Julia away from the pump, if she is tempted, until I have the chance to dismantle it.

Dinner was delivered at six o'clock as usual. Mark called, "Julia, dinner's up," as he always did.

These routines were familiar now and comforting. They were also stifling. Julia ate the shepherd's pie that Mark had made. It tasted good. Would she still be able to cook when she left this room? As she ate tears rolled down her face. She was mourning the brief wild period of her life which she was leaving behind.

Earlier she had managed at last to unlock the window. A feat which bad Julia would not have had the patience to do. Now that Mark was in for the evening and she had finished her dinner she opened the window. She looked out over the garden and breathed in the air. She closed the window again, lay down on the bed and stared at the ceiling as she thought about her life.

Childhood had been a fight for attention with her siblings. Julia had pretty much given up the fight at the age of five when she couldn't compete with her brighter older sister Kelly or her drama loving younger sister Sarah. Her school and college years had involved a battle with mediocrity. She had come out with reasonable qualifications through sheer dogged hard work.

A series of bossy overbearing friends had blighted her school years and reinforced her lack of self-confidence.

Working in the solicitor's office had been OK. Julia had found a place where quiet hard work had been appreciated. She was surrounded by people in their thirties or over and could see her future when she looked at the older secretaries still doing the same job after twenty years.

She had no ambition to be any different she just accepted her fate.

Then Julia had met Mark. Not exactly a knight in shining armour but he had rescued her from her family and offered her a future and hope. The first two years of her marriage had been happy. She was building her nest and getting ready to have a family. It never happened of course, and from the first indication that she had fertility problems she began to fade away.

What had she become in the last few years? A shadow of a person who barely existed. She took no pleasure in her life and merely went through the motions every day. Poor Mark eating all those terrible dinners.

A storm was raging outside. Rain had continued to pour all day. Julia thought it was a suitably dramatic backdrop for her deliberations. She went over to the window and opened it.

Chapter 67

Julia didn't remember actually taking the decision to climb out of the window. Once she was walking across the room her momentum carried her on until she was halfway out. A moment of hesitation and then she manoeuvred herself so that she was hanging by her hands from the window ledge and then she let herself fall. It wasn't a good landing. She landed on one foot and then fell to one side.

Her arm was broken. Julia didn't need a doctor to confirm that. The sound of a snap and the intense pain were all the proof she needed. Her ankle had been twisted on landing as well. It was two o'clock in the morning and pitch black as Julia made her way, very slowly, towards the pump. She did not know about the hole Mark had dug and took a step near to the pump and found no ground to plant her foot on. It was too late to adjust her balance which was already impaired due to her injuries. She fell into the pit which was now filling with water and her hand found a skull.

There was now eighteen inches of water in the hole and it was still raining. Water was running down the sides making them slick and muddy. Julia couldn't get her feet under herself and she couldn't pull herself up. She had felt the skull as her hand went under water and she was now becoming aware of the other bones. Strangely fascinated she felt the rib cage and followed the spine down towards the pelvis and felt for the legs.

A calmness had crept over Julia despite her dire circumstances. She knew she would die in this hole and she really didn't mind. She had existed for thirty-nine years but had only really been alive for one. She thought of her family and then she thought of Mark. Poor loyal, thorough, infuriating, dependable, lovable Mark.

In the morning Mark took Julia her breakfast. He called to her as he reached the room but there was no reply. He bent down to push the plate into the room and felt a breeze on his hand. It took him a moment to realise that if there was a breeze then the window must be open. He was concerned and concern rapidly turned to panic. He fished the keys for the padlocks out of his pocket, he carried them everywhere, and went into the room. As he feared it was empty.

He was running down the stairs; he flung open the back door and ran across the lawn towards the pump. Mark stopped at the edge of the hole he had dug and looked down. Julia was face down in the water and not moving. She was wearing her silk blouse, the one that she had stolen, and jeans and had nothing on her feet. How strange that he should note what she was wearing he thought. He looked at her shaved head and instantly he couldn't recall what she had looked like with hair.

Back inside Mark was picking up the phone. Mark was dialling 999. Mark was crying. The police arrived and found Mark sat at the kitchen table in a state of shock. They asked where the body was and he pointed to the garden, unable to speak as he started crying again. "Can you tell us what happened?" a policeman asked. How did he begin to answer that? I locked my wife in a bedroom because she was addicted to water from a pump and she climbed out of a window, fell into a hole that I had dug and drowned. That was the gist of the story. It sounded ridiculous to Mark as he told it. What the hell would the police make of it? Oh and there was a skeleton already in the hole.

Mark made another phone call, this time to Kelly. It was difficult for her to discern what was going on. Mark was rambling about a hole filled with water and Julia climbing out of the window. She finally understood that Julia had fallen into the hole and drowned. The police were at the house and they had found the skeleton. She would get to him as soon as she could. She would phone her parents Bob and Penny.

It was a long morning filled with dozens of people, some in those white coveralls, trooping through the house and garden. At some point Mark realised that he was under suspicion and fear interrupted his grief. He was utterly overwhelmed and when they asked him questions now he couldn't even speak. He sat shaking his head and crying.

Thank God Kelly had arrived. She was a very capable woman and, despite her own grief, took control of the situation. She confirmed to the police that Mark's story, although bizarre, was true and she had known about the detox program. He had also told her about the skeleton which he had found the night before. She had spoken to Mark every day about Julia's condition. He was sure that he was near to curing her of the addiction, which made this tragedy even more sad.

Chapter 68

Nothing ever happened in the village. Now there were two bodies in the same garden in the same hole. The medical examiner finally approved the removal of Julia's body and then the process of investigation started again for the skeleton which was underneath. Mark caught snippets of conversation as he sat with a cold cup of tea in front of him. Every now and then the cup was removed and replaced with a new hot one but he didn't drink any.

Doctor Young had arrived and was talking to the police about Julia's medical history. He was there to check on Mark but had been keen to endorse the view that Julia was in a disturbed state of mind. The police were everywhere in the house. Collecting things from the bedroom and even taking Mark's wall chart showing the water reduction plan. Kelly spoke to every person who passed telling them that this must have been an accident. Mark would never ever hurt Julia.

The detectives stood at the bedroom door looking at the hasps and the padlocks. Inside the room a forensics operative was dusting the outside of the window ledge for prints. This was the most extraordinary crime scene they had ever attended. The medical examiner had deferred judgement on Julia's death until an autopsy had been carried out. The skeleton, according to him, was old and had been there a considerable time.

The two detectives were running through the scene again. The window of the bedroom was open and the technician had found fingerprints on the windowsill. They had looked at Mark's water reduction table with bemusement. An organised rational approach to a most irrational problem. Surely he could not have actually believed that his wife was addicted to water from a borehole? What did he think was in the water? The skeleton was many years old but made everything they had discovered more confounding.

It had been difficult to get any sense from Mark who was obviously overcome with grief. Not the standard reaction of a murderer. When the detectives finally grasped what they were being told discussion turned to the water. Mark had managed to produce a report from the local authority about the borehole and had rambled about some home testing kit he had used.

They took the report away with them but were not entirely sure why it might be relevant.

The standard line about not leaving the area without notifying them was relayed to Mark that evening when the police finally left for the day. Tape was draped around the pump area and its bright yellow colour caught Mark's eye whenever he passed the window. "Kelly, we were so close. One more day and she would have been free of that water and back to the old Julia."

Kelly made another pot of tea.

Penny and Bob got a call from Kelly giving some more details about Julia's death. "It was an accident. A terrible accident."

Her parents were bewildered by the story of her incarceration and her escape. "Why would he lock her up like that?" they asked again. Kelly took a deep breath and went over the story once more. For all their bewilderment they knew that Mark would only take such action if he thought it was absolutely necessary.

The village was agog with news of the tragedy and at Pilates class the middles conducted their own inquest. "So she drowned in a hole which Mark had dug in the garden and in the hole was a skeleton." They shared their memories of Julia. The good ones and the bad ones.

All of them agreed that she had been unbalanced in some way. All of them had been contacted by the police who were building up a picture of a highly disturbed woman. A woman who would climb out of a window in the middle of the night?

The manner of Julia's death and the extra drama of the skeleton meant that it wasn't just the village that was interested in what had happened, it was the country too .Reporters had started arriving within hours and there was barely anyone left in the village who hadn't been questioned about Mark and Julia. Zoe had granted an interview to one of the broadsheet newspapers about her dear friend Julia and her problems. Faith had resolutely refused to get involved. She felt the guilt of not helping her friend all over again and more profoundly.

Details of the findings on the skeleton appeared first. It was the body of a woman aged between twenty and thirty and was approximately one hundred and fifty years old. The woman had likely been murdered. There was evidence of repeated blows to the head. Her identity was unknown but local searches into any records of that time may help to solve the mystery.

Donna read about the skeleton and thought of the story of the lovers Elizabeth and John who had lived in the cottage in the 1850's. Maybe their romantic story hadn't ended so happily after all? Barry thought she should tell the story to one of the newspapers and earn a few bob.

A few days later the story of Elizabeth and John was printed. It was the perfect story. Rich young wife of an older husband running away to her young farm worker lover only to end up murdered and buried in the garden of their love nest. It was accepted by the public as the truth even though it had not been verified.

Chapter 69

The police gathered statements from every acquaintance of Mark and Julia and a consistent picture emerged. They were a loving couple who had been married for ten years. Julia had suffered some kind of mental breakdown, they couldn't ever believe the water addiction story, which led to bizarre behaviour. Every person questioned had been eager to stress that Mark would never have hurt Julia.

When the police spoke to the medical examiner he revealed that Julia had injuries which confirmed that she had fallen from the window. The police would have to work out if she jumped or was pushed. There were no chemicals or drugs in her system. In general, she had been in very good health. He thought a possible explanation was that she had fallen into the hole and, being injured, had been unable to climb out. There were no bruises to suggest that she had been forcibly held under water.

There was no financial benefit to Mark from his wife's death and everyone they had spoken to, friends and family, had been staunch in their support of him. He would never hurt his wife.

There had however been many reports of Julia's erratic behaviour and binge drinking. She had even been referred for therapy. The police invited Mark to the station for an interview to record his version of events.

He had never set foot inside a police station before. The fact that Mark was there made him nervous. The strange story he was about to tell them made him even more nervous. He had made a garbled statement immediately following Julia's death and the police now wanted him to repeat the story and answer supplementary questions. In an interview room, having been read his rights, he was faced by two police officers who were recording their conversation. No pressure then.

Taking a deep breath Mark went back to the early days of Julia's addiction. He outlined the change in her personality from a shy socially awkward lady to a foul mouthed drinker who upset everyone with her cruel gibes. He included the episodes of shoplifting, being drunk during the day and alienating her Pilates crowd. He then gave them details of the two instances when she had shown withdrawal symptoms. He had referred her to the doctor who had referred her to a therapist who had been unable to help.

It was with desperation that he had finally devised a plan to lock Julia up and undertake a detox. He wept as he described the gradual reversion that Julia had gone through and how she was once more becoming her quiet self. The scheme would have been completed on the twelfth day, the day her body was found. The police officers were still sceptical of the story. It was hard to believe that somebody could be addicted to water but the consensus among those who knew Julia was that a drastic transformation had taken place.

The officers were particularly interested, of course, in the night of Julia's death. This was the part where Mark could not help them. He had delivered her dinner at six o'clock as usual and had spoken to her before he went to bed at around eleven o'clock. No, there had been no indication that she was disturbed or contemplating escape.

She had been very calm and had talked briefly about how she was getting back to normal. There had been days when she was racked with guilt by what she had done but she seemed to have moved on to a placid acceptance.

Every moment of that night up to when he went to bed was recorded in minute detail. The weather conditions, loud rain and high gusts of wind, were noted. They asked Mark about the plastic shards that she had used to pick the lock. They asked him about the reason for digging the hole round the pump in the garden. They asked about her shaved head. That upset Mark again. When they got to the end of the story they went back and checked everything again.

Exhausted Mark was finally released and told to report back to the police in a few weeks' time.

Mark was told, eventually, that he was no longer under suspicion. At that point grief hit him all over again. It was as if he had suspended his mourning while worrying about the police investigation and was now free to resume. He looked out of the kitchen window and could still see a small piece of crime scene tape fluttering in a bush. He must go and remove it at some time.

The inquest brought new torture as the details of Julia's death were revealed and the story of her last night pieced together. The autopsy revealed that she had a broken right arm and had damage to her right ankle. This was consistent with a fall from a second storey window. It would have been difficult for her to walk. On the night that she died the heavy rain had not only collected at the bottom of the hole where she was found it had also made the sides extremely slippery. With her damaged arm and ankle, once in the hole she was unable to get out.

The water in the hole had been about two feet deep, it was estimated, so she probably drowned after succumbing to exhaustion from trying to escape. It was ruled an accidental death and it was noted that the balance of her mind was disturbed at the time. The inquest reawakened interest in the story and several newspapers tried to link the deaths of Elizabeth and Julia one hundred and fifty years apart.

A newspaper story from the time:

WEIRD WATER IN WELLHAM

When Mark and Julia Stone moved into an idyllic cottage on the edge of the charming village of Wellham they had no idea of the tragedy to come. The attractive couple bought the cottage, valued at £400k, for its privacy. It is surrounded by gardens and situated down a private lane.

Mark an architect, aged 41, and Julia a housewife, aged 39, were soon enjoying village life and partaking in local activities. Mark joined Fernbarrow Golf Club, fees £1250 pa, and Julia took Pilates classes at the village community centre.

Julia Stone was suffering from depression when they moved to the cottage. She was quiet and withdrawn and her husband hoped that the peaceful cottage would be soothing for her.

Before she started venturing into the village Julia spent her time in their home's beautiful garden.

It was in a corner of the garden that Julia uncovered a Victorian water pump and she began enjoying water from their private supply. Records show that the couple called in the local authority to carry out a risk assessment and test the water. All indications were that the water was safe. Those tests could not possibly uncover the bizarre truth of the pump supplying that water.

Over the course of the next year Julia underwent a complete change of personality illustrated by outrageous behaviour. She would drink to excess, insult her friends and there were rumours of criminal activity such as shoplifting.

Claire Rowley attended Pilates class with her and said, "She was very shy when we first met her but she changed and became confrontational."

Emily Fuller another class member added, "She was so rude sometimes and you never knew what she would say next."

Julia became addicted to the water and in a desperate bid to help her beat the addiction her husband locked her in the bedroom and tried to wean her off. Police reports show that padlocks were found on the bedroom door. There was also a chart showing the measurements of water she was allowed each day on a reducing scale.

Determined to stop the supply of water Mark had dug out a trench around the pump ready to dismantle it. In the trench, to his horror, he found a skeleton.

Catastrophe was not far away as Julia, unable to beat her addiction, climbed out of the first floor window in a last ditch attempt to get to the pump. The fall from window caused her to break her arm and twist her ankle. She escaped in the middle of a rain soaked night and made it to the pump only to fall into the trench and tragically drown, being unable to climb out due to her injuries.

There were now two bodies in the garden of the cottage. Mark, who was under suspicion for murder initially, made the gruesome discovery the next morning and contacted the police. The inquest ruled Julia Stone's death an accident but noted that the balance of her mind had been disturbed.

The skeleton was that of a female aged around 20 and had been buried for 150 years. Skull fractures showed that this Victorian lady had been murdered. A local legend supplied a name for the victim. The story of Elizabeth Hunter, lady of the manor, and her lover John, a farm hand, had been passed down for generations. Elizabeth left her older husband Henry, a wealthy gentleman farmer, for John. It was always thought that they had run away together but the find suggests that Elizabeth met a violent death at John's hands.

Many questions have been asked about the coincidence of two women ending their days in the same trench. Did the skeleton of the murdered Elizabeth have a malign influence on the water which flowed through the pipe next to where she was found? Was Julia doomed from the moment she took her first sip of the tainted water?

There have been many examples of evil spirits being linked to objects. Dolls, mirrors, paintings and even chairs are said to have shown signs of possession. This case was very different because it involved a spirit having an effect on an element, water, which when consumed caused profound changes. The water pump has become the subject of great interest among paranormal investigators and mediums.

Eric Chivers, an expert on the supernatural, has been to the site of the pump and said that he felt the presence of a malevolent spirit lurking there despite the skeleton having been removed. He used an electromagnetic fields meter and recorded anomalies around the pump area. "This is a fascinating possession," he said. "I am glad that I have been able to visit the area and take readings and photographs to document this phenomenon." He plans to research the history of the cottage to see if any further incidents of altered behaviour have been recorded.

A noted medium Marie Grey also visited and claims she made contact with the spirit of a young woman when she approached the site of the pump. She asked the spirit to leave and cleansed the area by burning sage. "This was a very angry ghost. Her life had been cut short by a cruel man and she wished to embolden downtrodden or insecure women so that they did not meet the same fate as her. I think she would have been an interesting character to meet. I asked her to move on to the other side and I hope that she has now gone."

Whilst we may never know the truth of why Julia Stone underwent such a complete personality change many believe that the water was a factor. Two young women ended their days in the exact same location. This must have been more than a coincidence. Julia's husband certainly believed that the water affected her and took drastic action to free her of her addiction to it. He has only spoken to the police about his wife's death and declined all requests for an interview.

In a statement by Mr Stone, read out after the inquest, he asked that he be given privacy and be allowed to grieve the loss of his wife in what was a dreadful accident. He understood that people were interested in the story because of the discovery of a skeleton at the same time.

Unfortunately, this had led to numerous incursions onto his property by members of the public who wanted to visit the scene. He would now be taking steps to remove the pump and hoped that this would deter further trespass into his garden.

Mr Stone asked us to make clear that he had not requested either Eric Chivers or Marie Grey to attend his property and that they had viewed the pump from an adjacent field.

Chapter 70

Guilt, regret and anger took their turns wreaking havoc on Mark. One more day, he kept thinking. One more day and that damned pump water would have been completely out of her system. He had locked her up for the last two weeks of her life, was another haunting thought.

Why couldn't she hang on one more day? Had she chosen the water over him?

The weight of the remorse Julia had felt for her actions must have played a part. Unable to cope with the hurt she had caused she had chosen the water because it would obliterate her guilt. This was the story that Mark settled on. It was the least damaging result for both of them. She had been too good to live with what she had done and he had not been entirely to blame.

The garden had become a source of curiosity. He would glance out of the window and see people in the field next to the house peering at the hand pump which stood defiantly at the centre of the hole. They would take out their mobile phones and cameras and take a picture often with them smiling in front of it.

Initially Mark had wanted to get rid of the cottage, but the site of two deaths, he was told by an estate agent, was a hard sell. He was glad in the end that he had stayed. Julia had been happy there. Those few blissful months last summer when she was more confident but not too far gone were what he clung on to. He had bought the small dog that he had imagined Julia walking as company for himself. He couldn't help but smile when it gambolled about the garden. He was desperately in need of a reason to smile nowadays. The garden held memories of Julia happily at work but was also home to the source of his misery. He had to finally do something about that pump.

The hand pump was removed and Mark had specified when he had scrapped it that it was to be melted down and not sold on. The pipe was cut back and capped as originally planned and to ensure that it was never used again the area was filled. A level plain grey square of concrete now marked the place where the pump had been. An homage to the architecture of Mitchell and Mitchell.